The Empress's New Lingerie

The Empress's New Lingerie
and Other Erotic Fairy Tales

Bedtime Stories for Grown-ups

Hillary Rollins

Three Rivers Press

New York

Copyright © 2001 by Hillary Rollins
Published by arrangement of Hillary Rollins and becker+mayer!

Published in the United States by Three Rivers Press, an imprint of the
Crown Publishing Group, a division of Random House, Inc., New York.
www.crownpublishing.com

Three Rivers Press and the Tugboat design are registered trademarks of
Random House, Inc.

Originally published in hardcover in the United States by Harmony Books,
an imprint of the Crown Publishing Group, a division of Random House, Inc.,
New York, in 2001.

Library of Congress Cataloging-in-Publication Data
Rollins, Hillary.
The empress's new lingerie and other erotic fairy tales: bedtime stories for
grown-ups / by Hillary Rollins.
   1. Erotic stories, American. 2. Fairy tales—Adaptations. I. Title.
PS3618.O55E46   2001
813'.6—dc21   2001024769
ISBN-13: 978-0-307-23878-8

Design by K. K. Arnold

First Paperback Edition

146470499

For "Lawrence Parks,"
who has given me the gift of eroticism,
and for "Lulu," who has blessed
me with fairy tales.

Acknowledgments

Many thanks to Shaye Areheart for her praise (and her patience), to Andy Mayer and everyone at becker&mayer! for their continued support (and their patience), and to Barbara Hogenson for being the kind of agent I am proud to call a friend.

Looking-glass,
Looking-glass,
on the wall,
Who in this land
is the fairest of all?

———

From "Little Snow-White,"
from *Household Tales,* by Jacob and Wilhelm Grimm

Contents

The Empress's New Lingerie

Red

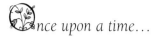*nce upon a time...*

...there was a young girl who lived with her mother near the edge of a forbidding wood. She had talc-white skin, lips the color of apricots, and a blazing head full of curls so coppery she was known as Little Red Riding Hood. But as she grew from a child into ripening womanhood, the heavy, shifting dunes of her breasts and the swell of her rounded hips belied the name "Little." She became simply Red.

The time had come for Red to enter the dark forest and venture forth without the company of her mother or any other protector along the path.

"You must carry these succulent treats to Grandmother's house," said her mother, handing the girl a laden basket. "And mind you, don't spill your treasures into the lap of some stranger along the way!"

Red started to protest, but she was hushed by a volley of teasing tongue-clicks.

"Uh uh uh, don't you deny it, young lady. I've seen the way your hips sway when you walk to market. I've seen the way you yield to the caress of the wind on your thigh or the sting of icy water on your hard little nipples when you bathe in the stream. These days you are about as likely to stray from the path of propriety as any wicked girl in the world, are you not!?"

It was true. Ever since she'd become Red she found herself unable to control certain impulses that made her blush with shame. The changes in her person—the tightening inward of a cinched waist in contrast to the sudden, unruly voluptuousness of belly and chest; the appearance of a natural and exotic perfume that rose from the folds of her breasts and armpits; the weighty, drawing, languid sensation (almost pain, but more exquisite) when, each month, her engorged womb filled and then emptied in a terrible, rhythmic flow—all these forced upon Red a new and disturbing sensitivity that plagued her day and night. She found herself suddenly aware of her own firm buttocks, her purple-dark slit and arching spine, until she had to seek private places behind the larder or under humid quilts at night to repeatedly, in a frenzy of flying fingers, seek relief from the burning self-consciousness.

But these secret acts, which always began in breathlessness and climaxed in a wash of pleasure, were inevitably followed by a sense of let-down and loathing that clung to her like a poisonous mist. She could not fully satisfy her cravings by herself. She yearned to enlist the aid of something or someone else to quench these internal fires. Yet here she was, all alone except for her decrepit mother. And now the old woman was compounding Red's wretched loneliness by sending her off, without benefit of friend or companion, on a tedious journey to Grandmother's house. It was too cruel, really. But perhaps it was exactly what she needed—something practical, something active and ruggedly physical to do—that might stop her from mooning about in a perpetual state of agitation and discontent. Maybe a vigorous walk in the woods would exorcise the demons that drove her inexorably to those desperate acts of sensual self-indulgence.

And so Red set off down the forest path, clutching her overflowing basket of luscious sweetmeats to her even sweeter bosom....

———

After a short while the pine-needle-strewn path took an unexpected twist. It turned away from the sunny and orderly fringes of the forest into its brambled and moist, dark depths. Here the light was dappled by dense thickets, the air felt as if it were pressing too close in a savage, insistent embrace. Strange shadows leapt at Red's feet and the abrupt flutter of an untamed bird or the eerie vibrations of a million teeming insects caused her heart to first stop then race frantically as she crept further and further into the ancient timber.

Suddenly from behind a gnarled grove of walnut trees there came a low, suggestive growl and something terrifying leapt in front of Red. She froze. Was this some hideous animal that dwelled in the forest's depths? Slowly she summoned her courage and lifted her eyes to see whatever it was that loomed so menacingly before her. But instead of a loathesome beast she found a man. An extraordinary man, perhaps—with broad shoulders and gleaming eyes, a shock of thick silver hair that swept around his neck like a fragrant pelt and a dark, toffee-colored complexion that made her own alabaster skin seem splendidly frail by contrast—but he was still just a man. He smiled, flashing his teeth like stolen gems in a pawn shop.

"Hello. My name is Wolf. May I help you carry your basket?"

"No—no thank you," stammered Red. "It's not very heavy, really. Just a basket of treats for my grandmother."

But for reasons she could not comprehend, her entire body trembled. She shook as if she were chilled by a blizzard, yet her ears, face, neck, and groin were flushed with heat. This was worse than the drunken fever that overtook her during her naughty little games, for this confusion went beyond her private, self-centered ravings to catch the handsome stranger in its powerful wake, making the image of his face and sinewy body enlarge and quiver and swim before her eyes in an unsteady whorl.

Her breath shortened. Her knees could not bend to move her forward or backward on the sullied path. The man bent closer to Red and his salty, aromatic breath seemed to set her flesh on fire. Her hands could no longer grip the basket and it slipped to the ground. Sweetmeats and sticky buns and ripe, bursting pomegranates rolled this way and that, but neither Red nor the fire-breathing man seemed to notice. Her snow-drift cheeks blushed as crimson as her celebrated mane, then drained again of all color. She almost passed out. But instead of succumbing to the faint her body just kept repeating the cycle of shivering and blistering until she grew exhausted. Finally she sank to her knees on the mat of pine needles below. The beautiful dragon-man knelt to catch her.

"What is your name?" he whispered.

"Red."

"Red...ruby Red...cherry Red...." he moaned, as he lifted and cupped handfuls of her flaming hair in his fists. He kissed and nuzzled and even gently bit this cascade, handling each burnished lock as if it had a nervous system of its own.

Eyes closed, mouth slack with ecstasy, he slowly drew a curl across his upper lip to feel its silken texture. Then he opened his eyes and stared with a crazy intensity into hers. He spread his fingers wide, stretched to hurting, as they fought through the auburn tangle, preening and combing and playing almost roughly in the fragrant mass with a desperate fervor. Suddenly he let his fingers go limp and gently settle on her neck, barely touching the hidden whiteness with his fingertips until she felt her bony spine melt into a column of shimmering liquid.

These alternating caresses drove her mad. One minute he was hotly inflamed by the feel, the smell, even the grain of her tresses, and his strokes would grow more and more frantic as he tousled them about like she was a rag doll made solely for his pleasure. She could do nothing to resist; she was pinned to the spot as his roaming fingers and probing mouth toyed with her hair, neck, ears, lips, collarbone, always returning to nestle again in the blazing mane of hair as he sighed, "Red, my unplucked rose, my blood-colored angel...." It was almost frightening—she felt like a tiny, defenseless rabbit that had been caught, trussed up, slit open, and turned inside out to be stripped of its precious coat. But no one had ever worshipped her fiery ringlets like this before, and even as she feared it, she thrilled to his violent touch.

Then, just as she was becoming lit by the flame of his passion, he would cool, suddenly pulling back with a terrible sort of detachment as he wound one long lock of hair around his forefinger. Using her entrapped strand of hair like a lasso, he gently, slowly, tugged his prey closer and closer to his hungry lips. The kiss of this wild and wor-shipful Wolf man assured her that at last she'd found the one who could fulfill her and end her loneliness and self-obsession. Gratefully, she tumbled into his lair....

————

Wolf carried Red the rest of the way through the woods to Grandmother's house. When they arrived, the elderly dame was nowhere in sight. Wolf set Red upon the bed, stripped her of her skirts and undergarments, and laid bare her second crowning glory—the spread of redheaded curls that adorned her mound and fringed the edges of her crimson labia and pulsing, swollen clit. The sight of such a luxuriance of Titian pubic hair nestled against the plump whiteness of exposed belly and thighs made her lover salivate, so deli-cious did this strawberries-and-cream delicacy appear. Just as he was about to bury his face deep within she caught sight of his giant, sup-ple tongue as it curled and quivered in anticipation of the waiting feast.

"Oh! What a big tongue you have!" she cried.

"The better to eat you with, my darling Red!"

This frightened the tender Red. Eat her? What exactly could he mean? She struggled to get away from the fearsome tongue as it lashed about preparing to dive. When he'd kissed her back in the woods this organ had seemed quite normal—hot and wet and hungry, yes, but of average size. Now as he contemplated her unveiled sex, which was as moist and ripe as a Caribbean fruit, this very same tongue seemed to swell and grow to outrageous proportions, transforming from a velvet sliver into a gigantic muscular thing with a pointed pink tip waving about like a diviner's rod searching for a tap spring.

Just at the moment she was about to be devoured by this slippery snake demanding its succulent meal, she cried out. And as luck would have it, an intrepid woodcutter was passing by. He heard her desperate cry and burst through the cottage door to save her, but it was too late. Wolf had pinned Red's knees open wide and his powerful, beastly tongue was already burrowing deep into her flesh with a force and rhythm that seemed heaven-sent.

The woodcutter wanted to do something, he really meant to do something noble and brave to spare this young maiden from her gentle rape. But the sight of Wolf eating out the luscious Red left him weak and useless and unable to move. The knob between his legs began to swell almost as large as Wolf's tongue and he stood there like a fool, his ax limp in one hand, his penis erect in the other.

Now Red was no longer crying in fear. Instead, she was moaning low, throaty sounds of pleasure. Her eyes rolled back in her head, her eyelids began to flutter and close in a languorous sweep. But before she shut them entirely, she spied the randy woodcutter standing by the bed. When her eyes met his, it gave him the strength he'd been missing to raise his ax high above Wolf's neck. But before he could bring it down hard, Red murmured, "No, wait...."

And then, as Wolf's ravenous mouth had its fill, Red's appetite was satisfied beyond her wildest dreams.

The End

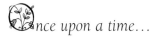*nce upon a time...*

...on a winter's day, a queen sat at her open bedroom window sewing a tapestry on a frame made of black ebony. She accidentally pricked her finger with the needle and three drops of blood fell upon the snow that banked along the window's ledge. The red drops looked so beautiful against the white snow that she said, "I wish I might have a child as white as snow, as red as blood, and as black as ebony." A year later, her wish came true: The queen gave birth to a daughter with skin as white as snow, cheeks as red as blood, and hair as black as ebony. She named the child Snow White.

But the queen died, and a year later the king took a second wife. This new queen was very beautiful, but she was also very proud and vain; she could not bear to think that anyone was as beautiful as she.

Now, this queen's most prized possession was a magic mirror. Every day she stepped in front of it to look at herself and say, "Mirror, mirror, on the wall, who is the fairest of them all?"

And the mirror always replied, "Fair Queen, you are the fairest of them all."

Sometimes she would use the mirror not only to admire her face, but to inspect and delight in the rest of her body as well—her pointy breasts, her wide hips, the soft down on her belly, and so on. In the privacy of her chambers she would take off all her clothing, place the mirror down on the floor, and then straddle the silvery disk so that she could catch a reflection of her beautiful crimson labia as it bloomed. Again she would ask, "Mirror, mirror, on the wall, who is the fairest of them all?"

And again, the mirror would answer, "Fair Queen, you are the fairest of them all."

Other times, when she didn't feel like being alone to fondle and fawn over her own charms, the queen would invite the king to visit her boudoir. On these occasions she hung the mirror in a special frame above the bed so that when he mounted her she could lie back and watch his pink buttocks pumping in rhythm to her sighs. This sight of the naked backside of the king, as he was reduced from a mighty monarch to a gasping, heaving servant of her desires, never failed to send the queen to the edge. As she crashed against the shores of pleasure she would catch a glance of her own face—twisted, flushed, and bloated with passion but still beautiful to behold—in her beloved mirror above the bed. And in the twilight that followed their lovemaking she would again whisper, "Mirror, mirror, on the wall, who is the fairest of them all?"

In a voice that seemed to mimic the breathless, spent murmurs of her royal lover, the mirror answered, "Fair Queen, you are the fairest of them all."

These words always made the proud queen very happy, for she knew the mirror did not lie. And with her husband sleeping soundly in their post-coital embrace, she thought there could be no end to the satisfaction and happiness her extraordinary beauty would bring.

———

But time passed, and as her stepdaughter Snow White grew up, the girl became more and more beautiful. One morning when the queen stepped in front of her mirror and asked, "Mirror, mirror, on the wall, who is the fairest of them all?"

The mirror replied, "Queen you are very fair, 'tis true, but Snow White is a thousand times fairer than you."

When the queen heard that she turned pale with rage and envy. From that moment on she could not even think of Snow White without feeling a bitter pang in her heart. Day by day her hatred grew until it gave her no peace.

At last she called her huntsman to her and said, "Take Snow White into the forest, for I never want to see her again." The huntsman did what he was told, leading Snow White so deep into the woods that he was certain she could not find her way home. The depraved queen assumed the wild beasts would devour her young ward, or that the child would die from starvation in the great, dark, snowy forest. But as Snow White wandered over sharp stones and past thorny brambles, looking for some exit from the thicket, she spied a light shining through the trees. With hope in her heart, she followed its beacon. At last she came upon a tiny cottage. Inside, everything was unusually small and in multiples of seven—seven little plates and cups, seven little spoons and knives, seven little beds all in a row.

The tiny beds were especially inviting to the weary girl, and she lay down on one for a moment's rest. Pretty soon she fell into a heavy slumber.

Later that night, the owners of the cottage came marching in. They were seven dwarves who spent their days digging in the mountains for gold. When they saw Snow White asleep on one of their beds, they didn't know what to do. They had never seen a young woman as beautiful as she, and powerful yearnings began to stir in their seven little cocks.

"We should wake her up, should we not?" one dwarf whispered.

"In a moment," said their leader, who could not take his eyes off the porcelain maiden in his bed. "First, a kiss. Just one kiss...."

The miniature man climbed up on the pillow next to Snow White's blood-red lips and leaned forward until his own were pressed against them. His mouth was so small next to hers it was as if a young child were kissing a grown-up lady, but there was nothing child-like in his ardor as he slipped his tiny tongue into her mouth.

"Oh!" cried Snow White, frightened awake by the dwarf's stolen kiss. "Where am I? Who are you? What are you doing!?"

But none responded, for by now all seven were stunned into a helpless kind of silence by the force of their sudden urges. All they could do was grunt and sweat and moan with longing, and several of them even drooled as they ogled the lush form that lay before them. She was gigantic from their point of view and as richly arousing as a virgin mountain of untapped ore. The lead dwarf was so overcome with lust that he began to cry like a baby as he fondled his stiff penis beneath his leather britches, and the sight of him suffering touched the heart of the innocent Snow White.

"There, there, don't cry, little man. Are you hurt? Let me see what it is that pains you there between your legs."

The weeping dwarf pulled out his erect knob and offered it up to Snow White like it was a fish on a hook.

"My goodness! No wonder you are crying. You are so small and this thing is so large and swollen! It must ache terribly," she murmured. "Here, let me soothe it."

As she stroked and cuddled the dwarf's now disproportionately large, thick cock the little fellow's pathetic tears turned to guttural groans and sighs of pleasure.

"See? You're feeling some ease already!" the princess noted. "Perhaps I should kiss it to make it better...."

She raised herself on one arm and leaned over ever so close to the dwarf's erection. She had barely grazed the head of the thing with her crimson lips when it reared back like a cannon and shot forth a gush of foamy brine. The discharge ran all into and around Snow White's open mouth, and it tasted like a mixture of fragrant forest pine and the salty black soil of the mines.

"Oh!" cried the shocked girl. Then she swallowed hard and forced a smile. "Well. I guess whatever was in there bothering you had to come out. Do you feel better now?"

The dwarf began to laugh with amusement and relief. "Yes, yes, much better. But my brothers are suffering so!" he pointed out. "Do you think you might help them, as well?"

"Of course," replied the angel of mercy, who was as generous of spirit as she was beautiful. One by one the remaining members of this band of miniature men stripped down and presented their rigid organs to Snow White to be rubbed and polished and nuzzled and suckled until the surging climax came.

Afterward, with seven flaccid, satiated pricks still wet with the dear girl's spittle, the dwarves lay about in the moonlight and asked Snow White to tell them her story. When she told them of how her step-mother sent her into the forest to die, it was their turn to show their generosity.

"If you'd like, you can stay with us for as long as you want and you shall lack for nothing," they told her. "We ask only that when we return each night, tired from our labors, you comfort and service us as you have tonight."

Snow White agreed. And for many days and nights thereafter, she lived quite happily in the tiny dwarf cottage with her seven randy companions. Sometimes they varied their evening ritual so that instead of each one receiving the lady's ministrations individually, they would lay her out upon the bed and en masse climb aboard her long-legged torso for a frantic group grope. One would place his penis in her mouth, another in her vagina, a third in her anus, the fourth and fifth would enter the dark groves of her armpits, and finally the sixth and seventh would violate the folds beneath her breasts. Then, in uni-son, they would ease themselves in and out of these sacred spaces until they had all satisfied their prodigious lust. All except Snow White, that is, for although she didn't mind these evening romps, she herself never experienced the pleasure of the game.

Meanwhile, back at the castle, the queen returned to her proud, vain ways. She was confident Snow White had long since perished and now she, the stunning queen, was once again the fairest in the land.

But when she queried her magic mirror, the answer came, "Queen you are very fair, 'tis true, but Snow White is a thousand times fairer than you."

Alarmed and furious, the queen swore she would hunt down Snow White and kill her herself. She discovered that the girl was residing at the home of the seven dwarves and was alone all day while the little men went to work. So the queen prepared a poison apple that looked so fresh and rosy whoever saw it could not help but crave a bite. Then she dressed herself as an old peddler woman and set out with a basket of wares—including the tainted apple—to pay a visit to the tiny cottage.

When she arrived, she knocked on the door and called out, "Lovely things for sale, lovely things for sale!"

Snow White invited the peddler in.

"I've many wonderful treasures to offer," the old lady croaked, "but none are as delectable as this juicy red apple!"

Snow White had to agree, and she immediately purchased the cursed fruit with a nugget of gold. But no sooner had she taken the first bite than she fell to the ground, apparently dead.

The wicked queen began to laugh. "White as snow, red as blood, and black as ebony, no one can save you now!"

When the dwarves came home that evening, they found Snow White lying on the floor with the bite of apple still in her mouth.

"She's dead!" the leader cried. "Our beautiful Snow White is dead."
The dwarves were despondent, for they had grown to love their precious concubine and dreaded returning to a life of lonely frustration without her gentle caress to arouse and relieve their bulging cocks. They laid her out upon a bier of sweet wood and were about to entomb her in a glass coffin so they could forever gaze upon her snow-white thighs, her blood-red nipples, her ebony pubis.

But before they did, the leader of the dwarves—the very same fellow who had once awakened the sleeping maid with his rude, intruding tongue—climbed up beside her for one last kiss. And as he slid the slippery eel between her parted lips, he dislodged the piece of apple from her mouth. With a start, Snow White opened her eyes. This time it was the dwarf's turn to startle with fear.

"Oh!" he cried. "You live!"

"Mmmm, yes...." drawled Snow White with a strange tone in her voice the little men had never heard before. It was the sound of a woman in heat—languid, full of longing, suddenly aware of her heightened senses and strangest desires. Her eyes, too, had changed. They were no longer the clear, feckless orbs of an innocent; now they shone with a knowing glint under the heavy lids, and their color went from the pure black of ebony to the smoky hue of the blackest fantasies. It seemed the poison apple had only poisoned her naiveté, melting her cold indifference to the sensual and summoning her to the flagrant possibilities for personal pleasure contained in her situation.

"Do it again!" she ordered the little dwarf. "Kiss me! All of you, kiss me at once!"

And the seven little men, happy that their dear girl was so very alive, were delighted to oblige. As seven little pairs of lips and hands roamed across the snowy field of her body, she suckled and savaged and sat upon seven not-so-little cocks until at last she had seven giant orgasms all in a row and lived happily ever after.

The End

Jackie and the Beanstalk

Once upon a time...

...there was a poor widower who lived in a little cottage with his daughter, Jackie. The only valuable possession they owned was a milk cow that had been their main source of food for many years. Each morning, when she thought her father was still sleeping, Jackie went out to the barn to milk the old heifer so they would have fresh cream for their breakfast. She never knew her father crept out of bed before she did and hid in the barn to secretly observe his little milk maid hike up her skirts and straddle her tiny three-legged stool. From beneath a blanket of straw he watched as Jackie firmly massaged the beast's distended udder to make the milk come in, then grasped the pendulous teats with a strong, sure grip to rhythmically, almost ritualistically, tug and release on the elongated nipples. As she leaned over a tin milking pail the buxom white globes of her own bosom spilled forward over the top of her gingham frock. For leverage she sat with her bare muscular legs splayed wide, feet planted firmly on the floor, calves and thighs flexing with the effort of supporting her broad hips and buttocks on the tiny stool. And the vision of his darling girl so full and open, so intent on her chore without a hint of self-consciousness, bobbing lustily against the hard wooden seat while pulling in and out on the cow's dangling lobes, made the furtive old man swell like a puffed up sausage. As she—swoosh, whish, swoosh, whish!—sprayed the hot, frothy liquid out of the beast and into the pail, her breathless father sprayed his foam into the fresh-cut hay in which he hid.

Now since this man and maid lived very far from the village and were so impoverished they could not afford a dowry, the father despaired of his daughter ever finding a mate. He feared she'd never feel the velvet touch of a lover's blistering organ nesting in her hands, mouth, or belly. He feared her only sensual experiences would be when she threw her head back and stretched her mouth wide to receive a stream of warm milk directly from the cow's teat, spraying the creamy liquid all over her face and neck, letting it drip down her cleavage and pool up in the tiny cup of her navel. Or when sometimes, because she thought she was alone and no one could see her, she would hoist up her legs on the beast's flanks and twist the flexible, fleshy teat toward her slit, aiming the fragrant stream at her little pink pleasure bud. The warm, wet pressure of the milk would pulse against her sensitive clit, churning her up again and again until she melted like butter. The old man could see his daughter thoroughly enjoyed these morning milkings, but he worried that it was not right for Jackie to be so intimate with an animal instead of a man, and he resolved to send the girl to market to lose the heifer and find a husband.

On the road to market Jackie met a butcher who was carrying some strange, brightly colored beans in his hand. She could not help admiring them, and when the butcher told her they were magic, she was persuaded to trade her cow for the handful of legumes. She ran back home to tell her father of the beans' supernatural powers.

"We can use their magic to make us rich and happy, Papa, to conjure up gold and silver and—"

"Oh, Jackie!" he cried. "How could you be such a fool? I meant for you to go to market and meet a handsome buyer who would give you a pretty price for that cow! These beans are worthless. There are not even enough of them to boil up for our supper. We shall surely starve." And my tender milk maid shall surely die an old maid as well, he thought. He tossed the cursed beans out the window.

That night Jackie could not sleep. "Tomorrow we will have nothing to eat," she thought, "and it is all my fault."

She began to weep, and soon she crept into her father's room to crawl under the covers with him for comfort, just as she had when she was a child.

"Oh, Daddy, what have I done?" the miserable Jackie sobbed.

Gently, slowly, the old man licked the salty tears off his baby's trembling face until she sighed and fell asleep curled against his warm chest. All night long he sought to soothe his dear girl, stroking her soft hair while she slept and fighting to keep from stroking her soft curves that pressed against him in the dark.

———

dew, and she prayed this slickness would ease the way for the lance upon which she was about to be impaled. Then carefully, deliberately, she lowered herself onto the rod.

At first there was no entry and she merely perched in a tottering sort of balance with her sticky nether lips spread flat against the top of the bulbous plant. It was as if she was sitting spread-eagle across a majestic redwood, so large was the pole she straddled and so small the opening she hoped to bury it in. But soon she began to rock back and forth, back and forth, rubbing her wet, open gash against the thing like she was oiling a leather saddle. And this polishing of the giant knob beneath her must have worked the magic that was contained in the beanstalk, for against all logic, the thing's enormous head somehow worked its way a few inches into her diminutive cleft.

Oh, the rapture she felt when it was lodged within! She squirmed and squealed and pushed herself down, down, down upon the perpendicular stalk and as she did her insides swelled and deepened and expanded until the whole shaft was submerged in her supple folds. In addition to filling her dark, inner space this voluptuous invasion also caused a tug and pull on the sensitive outer structures of her orchid-shaped organ, so that now her clit and labia were stretched and twisted into a state of unyielding arousal.

Her father may have despaired his daughter's fate when she traded the prolific heifer for those seemingly worthless beans, but he could not have known how much power their magic would ultimately have to please and satisfy his precious baby girl. If she had found her way to the market and sold the cow as he'd instructed she might have met a mild-mannered husband to share her bed. But how could the ordinary penis of some simpleton from the village ever compare to the magnificent vine that was slipping and sliding, bucking and braying inside Jackie now?

Up and down, in and out, the transformed maiden writhed until all at once the earth moved. Literally. For just as she reached the most explosive climax of her life, a stentorian voice rang out from somewhere below the clouds, crying, "Fee-ee-ee…fi-i-i…fo-o-o…fu-u-m!" And the miraculous beanstalk moved from its vertical orientation to a horizontal one. Jackie looked up from her precarious mount and saw that she was skewered upon the penis of an other-worldly giant, as handsome as he was enormous, who had just bolted to an upright position, tensed and braced for his imminent release.

"I smell the blood of an English—" he murmured in the last few seconds that felt like forever. Finally, Jackie burst into a second streaming orgasm off the excitement of watching the giant's tortured pleasure begin to erupt, and in concert they both finished his song.

"…CU-U-U-M!" they hollered, and the giant's wand exploded, blowing Jackie into the air by the force of a magnificent geyser and depositing her in a sticky pool of liquid on the other side of the clouds. Slowly she floated back to earth.

The End

Cinderella

Once upon a time…

…she stepped through the door, and in so doing trampled my heart until it was nothing more than a quaking thing beating like a wounded hawk in my breast. Most people assumed it was her striking beauty—golden hair, cat eyes, cheekbones as sharp as street knives, lips swollen with the juice of pomegranates and plums—that had me vowing to make her my lover and my wife. I did appreciate the lady's fine-boned countenance, riding high and proud above cream-colored shoulders and an impossibly cinched waist. But it was not the beauty of her face or figure that reduced me to this quivering goddess worship.

What then? Her soul? The gentleness of her spirit, the qualities of kindness and munificence that poured forth from her? I now know that she truly had such inner beauty, evidenced by the fact that she'd ministered to the needs of a doddering father, his evil wife, and two vain and selfish stepsisters without a whisper of complaint. Perhaps you think her a fool for allowing herself to be so used, for agreeing to cook, clean, and sweep the ashes from her family's barbarous hearth. After all, since the death of her mother, she was the rightful mistress of the house and should not have been reduced to the role of scullery maid. But it was out of her deeply caring nature, and especially her love for her elderly father who was too infirm to realize the depth of his daughter's humiliation at the hands of the she-devils who'd interpolated themselves into their lives, that the maiden felt she was duty-bound. Still, admire them as I might, it was not these attributes of goodness and charity that initially attracted me to my angel, for when I first laid eyes upon the girl I knew nothing of her circumstances.

That auspicious sighting occurred at the fancy-dress ball I hosted under the guise of entertaining the neighborhood—an affair I throw every year to share some of the fruits of royalty with my deserving subjects in gratitude for their loyal service and obedience. But this year's event was motivated by a more personal agenda: I dearly wished to find a wife. Of course I preferred not to advertise this fact as I thought it somewhat demeaning that I should be, in effect, shopping for a mate. But somehow all the eligible damsels in the province got wind of my intentions and a record number of marriageable lasses turned out, tarted-up and eager to "land a liege." With so many *jeunes filles* to choose from, you would think I'd discover my bride in no time. But truth be told, I have very...shall we say, "particular" tastes in women. And when a prince's tastes are particular, perhaps even a tad peculiar, it's not so easy to match him with his perfect princess.

That night I danced with girl after girl, hoping one of them would meet my requirements and ignite my desires. But no one even raised a spark. And it was not for lack of trying on their parts. Most ladies wore gowns so low cut that the edges of their brownish-pink areolas peeked over the top of the neckline, and I knew this was intended to make me grow rock hard and completely irrational. I knew, too, that they expected me to bury my face in their bosoms during a dramatic dip in the gavotte to take a surreptitious bite out of these flesh-apples pushed upward beneath their bodices like offerings at a banquet. So to satisfy their expectations, and perhaps their cravings, I ran my long tongue deep into each maiden's perfumed décolletage and nibbled with gusto on their breasts. I felt their nipples tighten and wrinkle up like ambrosia berries until the tips grew purple and throbbing. One after another, I would sashay my partners behind the camouflage of some marble column or velvet drapery and there I would greedily reach inside their gowns and pull their tits up over the scoop necks to suck on their protruding nipples with the grunts and sighs of a madman. As I pressed an insistent knee against the heavy brocade of their skirts, searching for the hidden "v" between their legs, I would run my tongue up their chests to the delicate arch of their necks, their chins, their waiting mouths, and then back down to their aching nipples.

This made some women delightfully agitated; they returned the pressure of torso against torso, they rubbed their thighs together beneath their sumptuous petticoats and squirmed in my arms like exotic fish. Others—those with the tiny, exquisitely sensitive, almost translucent nipples of a teenaged virgin—simply swooned when I tasted their delicacies, rolling their eyes back in their heads and collapsing in a seductively limp tangle in my dancing arms. I enjoyed administering these love bites, enjoyed seeing the milky complexions of the maidens flush red and bloom with shame and desire. But as for me, I felt no fire within.

Then she entered, seeming to float to the top of the golden staircase. She hesitated, surveying the undulating dance floor below, then slowly, purposefully, like a giant cat, stretched one long leg out from beneath her ankle-length gown. For just a moment before her descent, that extended limb hung poised above the first stair, and that is when she slew and felled me like a lovesick dragon. At the end of this shapely leg was a rosy, naked foot the likes of which I had only dreamt in my dark, secret little daydreams. The tender foot beckoned me to come to it, to sniff it and suckle it and venerate its arch and instep and tiny fresh-water-pearl toes with all the passion of a zealot....

Ah, but perhaps I've confused you or led you astray. I said the dear foot was naked, and you must be wondering what sort of a low-rent trollop comes to a ball at the palace with feet unshod and *au naturel!* My mistake. You see, I remember this foot as naked because I could see every curve and coloring of its perfect form. But this charming appendage was not actually nude. Rather, it was clad in a unique sort of footwear, a shoe that visually exposed all the vulnerabilities of the naked foot to an admirer's ravenous eye yet held that cherished nakedness encased in a clear coffin, thus keeping the foot aloof and always just slightly beyond his grubby reach! For this maiden's slipper was made out of glass—fine leaded crystal that rang like a church bell when heel tapped against heel—and it was seductively and maddeningly transparent as it gleamed in the light of the candelabra. All five toes were visible, like fat little piggies lined up for slaughter, but they were squeezed together and locked away behind their tiny glass enclosure designed to frustrate my overwhelming urge to bite them one by one. The shoes were shaped like standard dancing pumps, except for the fact that the heels were so extremely long, high, and spiky that they made my loved one tiptoe on the tender balls of her feet and forced her instep into a severe and exaggerated arch that could have curled itself around my throbbing penis. This extreme bending and arching of her supple tootsies had a superb effect on the rest of her lower extremities, forcing, as it did, the lithe, rounded calf muscle to flex and shape itself into its most feminine and enticing lines. I could see glimpses of this exciting lower leg, and sometimes even a tease of knee or thigh, whenever she lifted her skirt during the minuet or kicked out her well-turned ankle during the spirited ron-delais.

Oh, to prostrate myself beneath such a foot! To feel the smooth sole of that slipper grind itself into my heaving chest, to kiss the rounded toe of the pump and taste the neutral covering of glass while I could only imagine the rich flavor of hot, moist flesh that lay with-in its confines! I would massage my lady's exhausted calves and ankles after she'd been dancing all night long, I would anoint her fragile skin with fine creams and oils, I would clean between her toes with my tongue and mix my tears with exotic lacquers to paint her seashell nails. Then, to repay me for my devotion, my cruel mistress would dig the glass heel, like an icicle shard, into my spine and buttocks, roll my hardened but helpless organ between her heels, make me scream for mercy as she stomped all over my defiled royal personage....

But as suddenly as she'd walked into my life, she was gone. At the stroke of midnight, my high-heeled dream flew to the top of the palace stairs and ran out the door. I'd never even gotten her name. All I had of the extraordinary woman was one glass mule, for as she ran it slipped off her foot, flew through the air, and fell into my outstretched hands. The silvery glass, still fogged up by the scented sweat of her delicious instep, did not shatter. My heart did.

Who was this creature whose brutally beautiful feet had danced their way into my life, only to disappear as swiftly as she'd come? No one seemed to know. Every flat-footed nag in the neighborhood who'd shown up at the ball could be accounted for. But the mystery nymph with the crystal slippers seemed to vanish into the midnight mist.

And so I undertook to find my lady at any cost. I began an arduous journey, traveling from house to house with the matchless shoe, searching for the foot that could wear this trophy of my lust and love. Time and again I was disappointed. The shoe was either too large or too small for every instep I cradled during these frantic fittings, although many a lass took extreme measures to try to fit into the transparent pump. Some of them slathered up their chubby, stubby toes with cooking lard in order to squeeze into the slender box, others sought to stuff the shoe with tissue when they thought I was not looking so their scrawny and bunioned appendages would appear to measure up.

And several took pains to distract me from their inferior feet by giving me their audience sans undergarments. I would bend to place the shoe upon a maiden's left foot, only to find she'd extended her right.

"Oops!" she would giggle, then ceremoniously recross her legs, making sure that in the fanning motion of these limbs her flimsy skirt would be raised just long enough for me to catch a dark glimpse of hairy cavern and breathe in a whiff of feminine musk.

It was not that these teasings left me entirely cold; I could feel slight stirrings of desire whenever I had my face buried between some mademoiselle's knees as I tried to slip the shoe upon her provocative, dangling tootsie. But at no time were these vague arousals comparable to the ardor I'd felt for the feet at the fete—those sensual and dainty pink doves I longed to feel wiggle their toes against my testicles or drive their heel between the globes of my buttocks. And nowhere did the shoe fit.

———

I came at last to the final house, a modest dwelling on the fringe of the peat bogs. There I was met by a monstrous woman so anxious for one of her two querulous daughters to fill the shoes of the intended princess that she'd cut whole chunks of tissue off their repugnant hooves in order to cram them into the slipper! Alas, there was not a fit to be had in this pitiful household, and as this was the last cottage in my dominion, I despaired of ever finding my true love.

"Isn't there any other person in this house, my good woman?" I cried in desperation. "Some niece or cousin I've not yet seen?"

"The only other member of this household is my senile husband," the gargoyle-matriarch cackled. "And I doubt his gouty old foot would fit!"

But at that moment a sparrow of a girl, dressed in rags and clodhopper work boots and covered from head to toe with the black soot of cinders, crept into the room. She began to clean the fire pit.

"Who is that?" I asked.

"Nobody! Just a little gutter slut who mops our floors and licks our sandals clean—"

I cut off the crone with a sharp gesture of my left hand and with my right I held out the translucent high-heeled pump toward the blushing waif.

"Please. May I see your foot?" I begged.

She crept toward me and sat upon a wooden bench to loosen the laces of her preposterous boots. And then, as if in slow motion, she lifted out one perfect, polished foot that shone like a beacon in the firelight.

"Oh God," I sighed, feeling my head lighten and my groin tighten with the rushing blood. "My mistress, my princess, my love...."

I fell to my knees and began to kiss and lick every nook and cranny of that plump bit of flesh until it was covered in my slick tribute to her pretty pied and it slid effortlessly into the glass slipper for a perfect fit.

The End

Goldie and the
Three Bare Bachelors

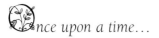 *nce upon a time…*

…there was a beautiful young girl called Goldie, named so because she sought perfection in all things and wanted every experience she had to be "as good as gold." Of course, life being what it is, Goldie was often disappointed and frustrated. Since she couldn't control the wayward acts of others nor get the rather chaotic universe to cooperate, she felt the ever-widening gap between her lofty idealism and the vagaries of an imperfect world.

And so poor Goldie lived with a chronic sense of hopelessness, a general sort of morbid dissatisfaction. Wherever she went, whatever she did, she was plagued by the sense that things were simply "not right." More than anything, she longed to have an experience that would live up to her gold standard, and with that in mind, Goldie set out looking for the perfect career.

———

The first profession in which Goldie sought satisfaction was that of culinary chef. Since food was such a fundamental pleasure, she thought she might find a truly basic experience of pure and absolute perfection in a job that catered to this fundamental need.

She enrolled at the Institute, studied hard, and when she graduated she was a gourmet epicurean of the highest order. She could make stacks of delicate blini, bowls of steaming pasta, strings of herbed bratwursts that crackled and spit when they yielded to the fork. This expertise made her extremely popular with the sort of men who are said to conceal their hearts at the end of the proverbial path through their stomachs.

One man in particular, Tom Fowler, found Goldie's way with a whisk especially alluring. Tom arrived at Goldie's house for dinner wearing nothing but a long trench coat and lace-up military boots. He was completely nude underneath the coat, presenting himself as a sort of tabula rasa on which the exotic cook might whip up any number of treats to satisfy her voracious appetite.

Goldie lay Tom out across her long dining room table, naked as a plucked turkey, with only his boots still on. First she bent his knees to his chest and tucked them under his arms, exposing his soft rump, puckered anus, and bristly balls. Then, with all the technique of an haute chef, she trussed up that giant bird using the laces from his boots to tie his hands to his ankles. Now he was ready for stuffing.

"Tom-Tom," she whispered in his ear, "I've got a gold medal recipe cooked up for you. By the time I'm finished, you'll be nothing but a soggy puddle of porridge."

And with that, she smeared her fingers with slick white lard and began to lubricate and ream his tight cavity with brisk strokes as if she were tenderizing a tough cut of meat. At first Tom winced in pain, but this quickly gave way to a deep, pleasant ache as his sphincter softened and yielded to the intrusion. When he was opened wide enough, she took small handfuls of a thick mixture of sweetmeats, roasted chestnuts, and bread crumbs and pushed them deep within his dark crater. Tom moaned with pleasure.

"Tasty?" she asked.

Tom couldn't answer because he was afraid he would explode. His bum was now packed with the stuffing; there was no way she could force anymore. But still she pressed on, shoving more and more of the savory mix up his hole. The heavy feeling of fullness in his pelvis made his cock respond in kind; it filled and expanded each time her thumbs dug into his hollow.

"I see you like organ meats with your stuffing, Tom-Tom." She bent over and took the velvet head of his penis in her mouth, running her tongue around it in a slow arc.

"Mmmm. The temperature tells me you're almost ready to eat. But the juices," she drawled, tasting a drop of salty fluid from the tip, "aren't running clear yet. We'd better wait a bit. I know! I'll baste your skin until it's good and crispy."

Out came a rubber spatula and whack! She smacked his up-turned buns until they were a lovely pink color. With every roasting his rump received from the pitiless spatula, his balls quivered like a pair of wattles and the throbbing knot of his dick swelled to the limit.

"And finally, the pièce de résistance," murmured Goldie, "the preparation of the breast meat." Slowly she poured hot, melted butter over his nipples and belly as he writhed against his truss bindings, trying his best to hold off his orgasm and not erupt in a saucy discharge all over her lacy Irish linens.

all the velvet, lacquer, chintz, and brocade. Not to mention the wall of leather whips.

"Provocative, isn't it?"

She spun around, stunned by the chilly ring of her host's voice. But this chill did not last long, for she saw he had somehow managed to get a fire started in the fireplace without her noticing he'd entered the room. The flames pitched warmth toward her with violence.

"Oh, Mr. Davenport, I didn't know you were—"

"Silence," he whispered, as he led her to the camel-backed loveseat.

Was it a spell cast by his unblinking eyes? Was it the effect of some hypnotic vapor rising off the burning logs? Or was it simply the surroundings—all that hard iron, soft velvet, and musky leather and their associations with lurid medieval rites of extreme sensuality—that had her so aroused? Perhaps now she would get to experience a moment of absolute perfection.

When they reached the miniature sofa, Davenport didn't offer his guest a seat. Instead, he bent her over the back of it, her head resting in the deep cushions while her waist straddled the rising hump. Her hips, legs, and buttocks were isolated and displayed as if they were separate from the rest of her body.

Quick as a ferret, Davenport had her legs spread-eagle, with each ankle tied to the polished wooden foot of the loveseat. He then shed his fancy Italian suit, lifted her tight skirt, and pulled down her silk panties, exposing the smooth cheeks of her ass. They shone like marble in the firelight, but when they caught blow after stinging blow from a rawhide horse whip, the quivering of these tender mounds proved that they were indeed vulnerable flesh.

Goldie cried out in pain, even as the delicious commotion between her legs grew with each assault. Soon she began to buck with pleasure as if she were the mare for whom the whip had been fashioned. But before she could reach her ultimate climax, Davenport spewed all over her buttocks, soothing the raised red welts with his fragrant balm, but, alas, softening his resolve to continue the frenzied act.

As he sank weak-kneed to the floor, she mumbled into the loveseat cushion, "Another satisfied customer." But what she thought was, "This chair is too hard."

Would any pursuit in Goldie's life ever provide her with the sense of satisfaction she so craved? It was beginning to seem it was not, but the intrepid Goldie wouldn't give up. She simply took a step back to regroup and figure out what went wrong. And what she concluded was that it had been folly to try to find fulfillment through careers of self-gratification. As a cook, she was catering to the gourmand's overindulgent pleasures of the palate. As a decorator, she was aiding a preoccupation with form and surface beauty, which was a luxury only the rich and privileged could afford. Maybe, thought Goldie, I should turn my attention to more altruistic pursuits. After all, didn't everyone say it was better to give than to receive? Perhaps the ultimate state of grace could be found in selfless service to others.

So Goldie decided to become a nurse. She went to the Institute, studied hard, and when she graduated she was a skilled R.N. able to inoculate, defibrillate, and generally ameliorate all manner of pain and suffering. This expertise made her especially popular with the sort of men who thrived on gentle ministrations and the healing touch.

One man in particular, Ted Ursa, found her way with a blood-pressure cuff particularly alluring. Ted was a patient in the critical care unit. For months he had been in a coma, the cause of which baffled the doctors. He had not been in an accident. He suffered no stroke. He was not the victim of a heart attack, overdose, or poisoning. He had not even been through a severe psychic trauma, at least not in medical terms. But Ted had suffered the loss of a love, and in his grief and pining, he simply slipped deeper and deeper into a profound melancholia until he reached a state of catatonia and practically ceased to function at all.

This would have been a tragedy had it happened to anyone, but it was especially sad to see Ted in such a state, for before his decline he was an enormously vital, virile bear of a man—barrel-chested, furry-headed, with powerful hands like paws and an even more powerful penis that swung, never less than semi-erect, between his brazen legs as he loped and sauntered through the world.

But now he lay in silent suspension, sapped of all his ferocious power, and Goldie felt an unusual degree of sympathy for the man. In fact, she was hopelessly attracted to him. Each day as she gave him his sponge bath she imagined what he would be like if he ever regained consciousness. Would his brow, now unnaturally smoothed by his tranquil condition, turn stormy with passion? Would those rich, full lips, ever so slightly wet and parted in their slackened state, draw into a furious grimace when he made love and then dissolve into an impish smile when he fell in love? She longed to know, as she gently soaped and cradled his flaccid organ in her capable hands.

But what was this? It seemed this recalcitrant organ, which had lain in a state of hibernation for so long, was beginning to be roused from its dormancy. His hot juices were definitely beginning to engorge the thick knob of flesh in her hands. Goldie started to knead his penis faster and faster with her soap-slick fingers as if she were administering CPR to a dying animal, in, out, in, out, the rhythm building as his cock strained harder and harder against her palms.

Before she knew it, she was rocking her pelvis in time with the massage, up, down, up, down, and feeling that deep, liquid spasm between her thighs. When his penis stood at its fullest erection, she was stunned by its animal proportions.

"Ooh, Papa Bear," she murmured, as she wiggled out of her nurse's uniform and climbed into bed with the patient.

Just as she was about to impale herself upon his rod, Ted gasped and opened his eyes! And the first thing he saw, after so many dark months in his strange cave, was this naked, panting angel of mercy. Their eyes met and, indeed, his sensual lips spread into just the sort of smile she'd imagined would signal his surrender to true and everlasting love.

They explored each other for several perfect hours, repeatedly climaxing in perfectly timed mutual pleasure, and between each perfect kiss, Goldie whispered, "Now this bed is just right...."

The End

Rapunzel

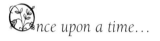 *nce upon a time…*

…I had long hair as thick and luxurious as a chenille stole. It hung down past my shoulders, back, buttocks, and calves, flowing almost to the floor. You wouldn't know it to look at me now with my inch of spiky fringe, but back then this seemingly endless growth was my pride, my glory, and the locus of all my feminine power. Otherwise beautiful women who had, alas, been cursed with thin, mousy hair seethed when I entered a party sporting forty braids coiled around my head in an elegant Byzantine pattern. Little girls of six or seven worshipped me, convinced that I was an actual fairy princess who had just stepped off the frontispiece of their storybooks. Small boys wondered silently about where I put that crazy ponytail when I had to go to the bathroom, then blushed and had their first ejaculations imagining me naked and squatting.

But it was the effect on men that pleased me most. When I danced and swung my hips from side to side the heavy pelt would sway in response and my partners were literally hypnotized by its undulations. When we made love, the snake-like strands flung across a man's chest or wound around his erect dick. My hair shot sparks of static electricity that stung and aroused, driving my lover to the edge. As he wrapped himself in my golden locks a man became completely entangled—not only in body, but in mind, spirit, heart, and soul. He exploded in rivers of pleasure, pulling out to spray himself into my tresses as if to mark them—mark me—as his own. And I let him pour himself into that thicket because afterward, limp and sapped of all his fury, he became a slave to its care and maintenance. He spent hours washing and drying, conditioning and pampering each strand, massaging my scalp with fragrant oils and begging for permission to gently brush my luxurious cascade with a hundred strokes each night.

Still, one day I grew weary of this game. My hair began to feel oppressive and like some ancient, vestigial organ that had long since ceased to be of use. In the summer I would sweat beneath its weight; in the winter the long hours it took to dry after a shampoo kept me housebound. And at bottom I never really knew if I was desired for myself or for my magnificent mane. I decided to cut it off.

Several days later I found myself riding the elevator to the top of a steel and glass office tower that housed the exclusive hair salon of a stylist known only as "Razor." If he had another name I'd never heard it, and his entire operation was cloaked in clandestine mystery. You couldn't get an appointment without knowing someone; he only saw one client at a time in private; and you had no say in the type of haircut you received—he simply gave you "the cut you deserved." By this I assumed he meant you got the style that most flattered your face, and I chalked up the odd phraseology to a simple language barrier. Razor came from some obscure part of middle or eastern Europe and was supposedly a deposed prince who had fled the Communists and come to America to shear the rich and famous.

I wasn't sure I believed all this, but his way with scissors was legendary and my precious locks could not be trusted to just any old barbaric barber. So I wrangled myself an appointment and prepared to let him clip. I knew I couldn't dictate the final length or shape of my style-to-be, but I hoped for a chic little bob and some bangs. What I got exceeded my wildest dreams....

———

Razor's shop bore no resemblance to any beauty salon, store, office, or other place of business I'd ever seen. The elevator opened directly onto a small, round room (the security guard in the lobby had to unlock a special button for it to take you there) and after the doors closed behind you the entire apparatus seemed to disappear so that when you looked around there was no visible exit. The walls providing this camouflage were of rough grey stone held together by a crude sort of masonry paste, a mixture of lime, earth, and straw. There were no windows or electric lights and it would have been pitch black if not for a small opening at the top of the cylindrical roof through which a pale column of sunlight slid. This beam threw very little illumination on the general area, focused as it was on the only piece of furniture in the room: a curious barber's chair situated smack in the middle of the floor like a throne. It had the usual foot and neck rests found on regular beauty parlor chairs and it swiveled and reclined like its standard cousin. But it was triple the normal size, both in length and width, so that when the operator moved it into the recline position it became more a bed than a chair! And instead of the usual vinyl or leather you might expect to upholster such a thing, this seat was covered in thick, luxurious black bear skin that seemed still redolent from the kill. At each corner of the contraption there was a solid gold handcuff that shone with an ominous glint in the pale ray of light. Other than this chair and a large mirror affixed to the wall, the room was as empty and bare as a tower of antiquity made to lock away unlucky virgins.

It was altogether spooky and a tad too weird for my taste—especially the handcuffs (since when did a hair client need to be restrained for a wash and blow dry?) and I would have fled right then and there had I been able to discover some means of egress. But, as I said, the fissure that had been the elevator doors seemed to heal up into the cold stone walls; I was trapped.

"Good evening," drawled an accented basso voice. "Please, have a seat." Seemingly from nowhere, Razor stepped out of the shadows. I was stunned to see he was so short for a man with such a resonant voice, and rather plain for a "prince," except in one respect: he sported more fur than his pelt-covered chair! This was not animal fur but his own thick, abundant hair. A mass of dark brown curls on the top and sides of his head seemed to expand in all directions like the locks of a feral child, while an especially lengthy tail tumbled down his back. His face was carpeted with a massive beard, leaving only two ice-blue eyes, a pair of sensual lips, and a set of high-gloss teeth to provide touches of smoothness to the craggy landscape. And it didn't stop there. I could see that his chest, arms, and legs were covered with a kinky dark growth that sprouted through all the openings of his clothing.

Normally I am repulsed by men with too much hair on their bodies, but the attraction I felt to this woolly beast was undeniable. It was as if each tuft on his muscular frame had a tiny magnetic charge, and collectively they pulled me toward him with a powerful force that made me ache.

"Why don't you come over here and have a seat?" he repeated. Not at all under my own power, I floated across the room and levitated into the barber's chair. I felt slightly faint from the rich odors of bear skin and masculinity that rose off my captor.

"I am not just stylist, I am artist with hair. You must receive proper cut not only for face, but for body, soul, spirit. Whole woman must be known to achieve supreme result, yes?"

And with that, Razor began undressing me, never taking his rapier eyes off mine. I should have resisted—I had come for a trim, not a tryst—but my fascination with his shaggy visage kept me pinned to the seat and the gentle, insistent pressure of his thick fingers as he unbuttoned my blouse and lowered my panties made me melt into the caress of fur that surrounded us. Before I knew it, I was nude.

Of course my hair was long enough to hide most of me from view, but now that he'd gone to all the trouble to strip me naked I expected my seducer to pull it back out of the way and fully expose me to his lecherous desires. Instead, he arranged it in layers of waves all around me, covering my face, neck, shoulders, belly, and hips and allowing the very ends of it to pool up between my slightly parted thighs. I was completely hidden under a tent of hair and the silky rustle of it against my skin was exquisite.

"First we must prepare area," he whispered as he slipped his hands between my knees and pried them apart. Then he strapped my ankles into the shackles, pinning my legs open wide. Positioning himself between my indelicately splayed legs, he began what seemed like a languorous massage of my clitoris and the outer lips of my vagina. I moaned, and relaxed into the rhythm, expecting to be manually coaxed to a simple, pleasant orgasm. But when I glanced up through half-closed eyes into the mirror I saw that Razor was not actually massaging me but was meticulously braiding the ends of my head hair into the wiry tendrils of my pubic hair! I gasped, and quicker than you can say "buzz cut," he caught my wrists in the handcuffs and locked them down with a resounding "click." He then finished weaving the two manes into one, spun the chair around so he was standing at my head and I could no longer see the mirror, and pushed the recline lever on the savage apparatus. With a violent bump the chair shifted into a prostrate position and I was laid out, my arms and legs stretched taut and my head, neck, and spine forced upward in a semi-curl because of the unusual tethering of the groin.

It seems like this awkward position should have been painful, but the stimulation of pulling action on my plump mound each time I moved my head drew an excess of blood to the area, treating me to delightful little spasms. If I could have just bobbed my head up and down a bit longer I would have exploded in a tremor of the most intense pleasure brought on simply by the tugging motion of the braided strands, the rubbing of lip against lip in my slick, wet labia. But Razor had a more elaborate treatment in mind. Suddenly I heard the terrifying "whir" of some kind of electric tool. A chain saw? A dental drill? My imagination conjured up the worst. Fortunately, my body was spared any gruesome demise, although my long hair was about to meet its untimely end, for the roaring implement turned out to be an electric shaver and its skilled operator began to steadily mow bald trenches across the top of my head with its oscillating blades. I could feel whole patches of my mane come undone from its moorings, could hear it fall away with a whispered sigh. With a voluptuous thrill, I felt my head grow giddily light and buoyant like a helium balloon and I savored the rush of cold air on my denuded scalp in such contrast to the heat in my slit.

When my entire head had been thoroughly shaved, Razor lifted my hair at its newly liberated roots and pulled it all forward so that it streamed down from my pubis, attached as it was by the intricate weavings there. He separated the mass into three thick cords and then braided those into a giant twisted rope that hung down between my legs like a ladder leading to heaven. He spun me around again and raised the chair back just enough for me to see my "new look" in the mirror: I was a vulnerable, tender, breakable flash of whiteness from head to toe except for the long braid hanging like a bizarre phallus between my legs, gently rubbing its downy irritation against my thighs. Clean shaven everywhere but there, I was more beautiful than I could have imagined, and as Razor massaged warm oil onto my smooth dome I felt a complementary friction deep within my cunt.

"You see?" he drawled. "You've been naughty girl with all that long hair on head. Using it for seduction, making men weak and emotional. Not Razor! Razor sees through cover of hair, sees real woman beneath. So I give naughty girl haircut she deserve, yes? Make her a naked angel, my naked angel, to possess…."

By now he was completely naked himself, his giant erect cock as purple, bald, and shocking as my shaved head, rising like a triumphant sword from the thicket that covered his loins. He mounted the chair, got on his hands and knees above me, lifted the giant braid that guarded the entrance to my insides like a curtain and grasped it in his teeth. Then rearing his head, he pulled my whole pussy up and out, opening the lips and exposing the pulsing pink inner flesh to his delicious assault.

———

Afterward, Razor washed me, inside and out, and treated me to a second shave down below, this time with scented foam and a gleaming, hand-held blade. He was so expert in his machinations he didn't even nick the skin and now I was left utterly nude everywhere: a satiated and smooth-skinned newborn cub curled up against the velvety fur of both bear and barber.

Now a few inches have come in, leaving me with this unkempt growth on both head and hind parts. So I'm off to the top of the tower for another appointment with my stylist-prince with his own special brand of "shear pleasure."...

The End

Beauty and the Beast

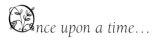*nce upon a time...*

...there lived a kind and handsome prince who was struck by tragedy when early in his life he lost his dear mother and was left to be raised by his father—a brusque and barbarous man who did not understand his special child. The king mistook the boy's acute sensitivity for weakness, thought he needed to be "toughened up" and properly seasoned in order to become a man. So when the prince was just thirteen years old, the king dragged him to the local whorehouse to simultaneously dispose of his virginity and his dreamy romanticism in one swift turn.

The house of ill-repute the king chose for this task was no cheery brothel filled with large-bosomed, warm-hearted women of experience who might carefully nurture and guide a youngster across that most sacred of lines separating youthful innocence from sophisticated manhood. This was a rough and ungainly place, reeking of whisky and soiled sheets, cooled by the foul winds of corruption and despair that blew through the cracks in the clapboard walls. It was populated by an underclass of dissipated prostitutes in whose false embraces and manufactured moans could be heard the constant tick of the time clock and the avaricious "ka-ching" of the cash drawer. The callow prince was forced to sample every sort of sexual congress with these whores, every lurid fantasy and lascivious posture, and because he was a young man with the healthy physical drives that accompany youth, his body responded in full. But his fragile soul shut down and mourned for its loss, for in his heart he longed for the kind of love-making that would express tenderness, caring, emotion, and, above all, sensuality. In this cheerless den each act was lustful and violent, a dance of mastery over one's subordinate, a contest in which the goal was possession, domination, and the finality of quick, self-centered orgasm. But where was the sweet give-and-take, the ardent passion, the spirituality and depth of meaning that was meant to back up these acts, meant to prolong, celebrate, and edify the process rather than shoot for the grunt-laden finish line?

The king thought these harsh episodes of counterfeit love would turn his tender child into more of a man; instead, they turned him into a beast. The gradual strangulation of his instinct toward slow-handed, languorous, sensual love made the prince grow bitter and doleful until he found himself completely transformed into the most repellent of creatures. Now his grotesque countenance and twisted form provoked fear and loathing in all he met, and the erstwhile, fair-haired boy was forced to flee the court and hibernate from society in a dark, deserted castle to live the life of a reviled beast.

The only link to the beauty and nobility of his prior self were the extraordinary roses he planted in the castle garden. The beast tended and nursed these flowers as lovingly as if they'd been his own chil-dren, and for the few hours each day that he mulched and pruned and watered the fertile plot, his princely nature would blossom alongside the buds. Soon he had rosebushes of such superior splendor that the handful of citizens brave enough to venture a peek through the garden wall returned home in rhapsody about what they'd seen. "The botanical beast" became a legend across the land. But everyone knew never to venture within those protective walls, and never, ever to pluck even one of the rare blooms. For when he was not tending his plants the cursed prince's demeanor would return to that of a feral monster, whose rages were even more legendary than his roses; the few who had dared to try and steal cuttings hadn't lived to see them bloom.

One day Beauty found herself walking along the road that led past the beast's castle. She'd heard the dire warnings against disturbing him in his grim habitat, but she'd also heard of the heavenly roses that flourished there. If there was one thing she adored more than anything in the world, it was a perfect rose. To keep such magnificent blossoms hidden away from others was, in Beauty's estimation, a crime against nature and a horror worse than anything the beast might confer upon her. She decided to climb the garden wall and pick the finest flower she could find to share with the outside world.

As she scaled the wall and came face to face with the famed rosebushes, she could not believe her eyes. These giant, succulent blossoms, redder than blood, pinker than a maiden's flesh, more yellow and white and orange and violet than the rarest sunset, were unlike any she'd ever seen before. They seemed to be almost animated, dancing and vibrating on their stems, deepening in color and perfume with every subtle quiver and opening themselves to the visitor's touch with the same dew-kissed yawn of a lover's slackened mouth in the afterglow. How could she even choose which rose to pluck? For each one she caressed seemed more perfect than the one before. Finally she settled on an especially superb bloom—an explosion of the finest crimson velvet at the end of an exquisitely slender, thorny, forest-green stem—and after drawing in a long, satisfying breath of its scent, she reached for its base and tore it from its moorings.

"Arrrgghhrrr!" roared the beast, leaping into view. Beauty recoiled, for he was uglier than she'd imagined. "You dare to meddle with my garden so now you must die!" the fearsome gargoyle announced, and he grabbed the cowering maiden in his giant paws and prepared to devour her.

"Forgive me, I only wanted one of the many spectacular roses you have!" she stammered, struggling unsuccessfully to free herself. "And I did not want it for myself alone, but to share with others!"

Forced to view him up close, Beauty could see through his gruesome exterior to a sadness within and realized the beast was really more pathetic than fearsome. She began to soften toward the fellow even as he threatened her life, and she turned her lovely face up to his terrible one to gently plead her case. "Besides," she said, "These flowers are not yours. You do not own them in the strictest sense, for while you have surely tended these beautiful buds only Nature herself can be said to have made them. And no man—or beast—has dominion over the glories of Nature. So to be blessed with Her fruits and then to hide them away from Her other attendants is to wound Her, is it not?"

Since the death of his mother no woman had spoken to the beast with such grace, such thoughtfulness, and certainly such kindness. The rude taunts and scatological chatter of the whores were the only feminine strains he'd heard since childhood, so this song of Beauty's was like a tonic. He knew he should have devoured her then and there, as he had the other impertinent thieves, but he wanted to hear her gentle, soothing voice again. He let go his grip and tempered his raging vengefulness.

"Perhaps that is so," he growled. "Perhaps I have no right to lock Nature behind my walls. But just look at me! Has Nature not wounded me more mercilessly than I She? Has that cruel mistress not warped and corrupted him who was once a prince and a gentleman into…into…this? A hideous beast whom no man or woman could love?!"

"That is not the handiwork of Nature," Beauty answered in her sweetest tones. "That transformation can only be the result of you forsaking Nature, your own nature. For I believe you are prone to the gentle passions of the softest goddess but instead have been a servant to the hardest of demons."

How could this Beauty know him so well? "You see all that when you look at me, lady?"

"When I look into you. Past the false and frightful face you show the world. I see all that when I see this perfect rose, which your loving nature has cultivated."

She bent to kiss the ruby-hued blossom she had plucked, and as she brought the talc-soft petals to her lips, a wondrous thing happened. The rose suddenly metamorphosed into a tall, lithesome, redheaded maid, as supple and stunning as the flower from which she'd arisen, and ardently returned Beauty's kiss.

"Blossom," sighed Beauty. "Mmm, my precious, precious Blossom."

The beast watched in awe, enraptured by their gentle rhythms, their abundant femininity, as together the two women sank to the ground and began to caress each other with tender touches punctuated by volleys of tiny kisses. Blossom, who was already fully nude, bent over the supine Beauty and carefully unfastened her bodice with long, tapered fingers that fluttered like white doves. She opened the panel of lace to reveal a pair of breasts so young and new and finely wrought they seemed like mounds of spun sugar topped off with their own miniature pink rosebuds waiting to bloom. The beast was used to mauling such a bosom, squeezing the globes in his grasping fists, but Blossom barely touched it. She sat back for a spell to regard the enchanting orbs as they were offered up to her until her eyes filled with adoring tears. Then she slowly lowered her head to allow one single teardrop to fall from each eye onto the perfect bull's-eye of each nipple. Beauty moaned as Blossom gently took the moistened nipples between her thumbs and forefingers and began to roll them around like lustrous agates in a bath of scented oil. As she continued to moan and sigh and purr with mounting pleasure, Beauty's long spine stretched and curved; she was a provocative cat in heat being petted and aroused. From this arched position she could reach her tongue up and out to wrap it lightly around the protruding nipples of Blossom's more womanly breasts, and Blossom eagerly fed her playful kitten these milky treats.

The watching beast breathed heavily. He felt his balls tighten and his prodigious cock swell and harden like a tree stump. But even as his sex grew hard, his features grew softer. By the time Blossom had helped Beauty remove the rest of her clothing and wind herself around the stem of her lover's flowering body, the beast was looking almost human. He watched as Blossom ran her thorn-like nails ever so gently up and down Beauty's back, not deeply or sharply enough to hurt her, but just enough to excite the sensitive nerve endings and bring on a heated flush. His fascinated gaze devoured the two as they took turns kneading and massaging each other's polished limbs, never in a hurry, never touching the sacred spot but concentrating instead on all the forgotten places: the backs of the knees, the soles of the feet, a neck, a brow, the cleft of the buttocks. For a while the two ladies just played with each other's hair, combing it through open fingers, twisting it into braids and buns, intertwining Beauty's rich, black pubic locks with Blossom's fiery strands. For another stretch of time they kept their eyes closed and their hands tied behind their backs, agreeing to explore the landscape of each other's bodies only by taste and smell.

Oh, how could they do it?! How could they keep from exploding, as he was sure he was about to do, keep from peaking and falling off that most treacherous of cliffs? But slowly, sensually, they continued to prolong this wonderful maddening tease, this mutual exploration of body and soul with no attempt to reach the main event. How he envied them, how he wished to join in their sensual gavotte. But he could not. To intrude his clumsy maleness into their sublime feminine circle would be too horrible. All he could do was watch, yearn, silently pray, audibly weep as the languid couple pressed breast to breast and mouth to mouth for what seemed an eternity.

At last Blossom began to carefully, tentatively touch and fondle Beauty's vagina. She started on the outside, making tiny little pats with her fingers along the swollen fault line of the lips, while all the while keeping a gentle, steady pressure on the hood of the erect clit with the heel of her hand. She never breached the opening of her own volition; rather, she coaxed and beguiled the delicate tissues until they opened on their own like a flower ripening in time-lapse photography. Only then did she slip a probing fingertip inside the silky slit to retrieve a drop of sweet dew. She licked this honeyed pollen off her middle finger and it tasted so delightful she had to have more. Down she dove into the fragrant bloom to drink of its nectar with the hungry, searching, vibrating tongue of a hummingbird. At that point Beauty's excitement began to really mount; her breath quickened, her toes pointed, her whole being tensed and released in tiny tidal waves. She was about to lose control, to catapult over the edge into the abyss. She gasped an inhalation as Blossom continued the rhythmic lapping and sucking, the pressing and releasing, the tongue and fingers against clit and lips. She exhaled a strangled sound of ecstasy as Blossom kept pecking and nibbling, kept rotating and stroking Beauty's swollen pelvic mound, dipping and pressing, kissing and licking over and over again for a suspended wrinkle in time that might have been minutes or ages. Finally, finally, it was too much and Beauty was crying and writhing and spasming her release under Blossom's velvet mouth.

And then, just as suddenly as she'd come, Blossom was gone. All that was left was the dainty rose Beauty had picked, that now lay in the humid pocket between her legs. As she recovered from her shattering climax, Beauty's eyes became clear again, filled with a profound peace and satisfaction. She turned these eyes to her voyeuristic captor. What she now saw was not the repulsive beast she'd encountered when she'd scaled the garden wall, but the handsome prince restored to his most civilized form. The only thing that was still animalistic about him was his engorged penis that bobbed and danced about like a puffed-up python. But now the prince knew better than to rush to his own wild completion as he once had. Instead, he lifted the fallen rose from its fragrant bed and began to use its whole nature—both the caress of its satin petals and the lash of its pointed thorns—to slowly tease and taunt and reawaken Beauty's passions for hour after hour of tender love. And, at last, beast and prince were united as one to live happily ever after.

The End

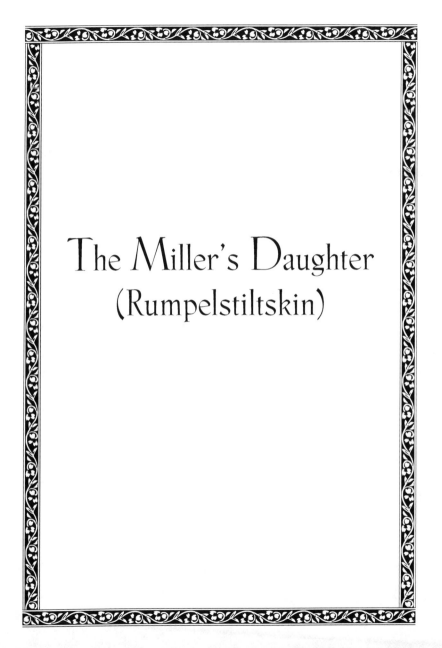

The Miller's Daughter
(Rumpelstiltskin)

Once upon a time...

...the miller's daughter was awakened in the middle of the night by a pair of invaders—two monster-men who seemed to be fashioned from knotty sinew and twists of chest hair. They wore leather hoods that covered their entire faces and had tiny openings only for their sinister eyes; in the distorting moonlight they appeared almost supernatural. If the miller's daughter had the time to catch her breath she would have screamed with all her might, but before she could exhale even a whimper of protest the larger of the leatherheads clasped a massive hand across her mouth and pulled her from her bed. She struggled violently, but it was no use; each desperate machination seemed to work her embattled limbs deeper into his grasp until her whole body was held and subdued by her captor. In this position, the tiny mouse pinned into submission by the giant hunter, she was powerless to ward off the thief's advances. He slipped an icy hand inside her gown. She was surprised at how gentle his touch was as he cupped one breast. But a moment later all mildness was gone as he grabbed the nipple between pinching fingers and tugged on it over and over again until it was stretched into a long, red, distended thing. At the same time he worked a bony knee between her legs, shoving the rough broadcloth of her nightgown deep into her crevice and grinding away in slow, deliberate circles until, despite her fear and rage, she felt the slick dew of pleasure gather between her thighs.

"It is useless to resist, missy, isn't it?" drawled the vile goon from behind his false face.

"And why would you want to?" piped in his companion in a mocking tone. "Until now you've been nothing but a humble miller's daughter. Tonight you are to become the king's personal property and his private delight."

His laughter was muffled and eerie due to the absence of a mouth opening in the gruesome mask. But as her darting eyes adjusted to the dim light she was able to make out a faint design burnished into the black leather in just the spot where there ought to have been human lips. It was the outline of the royal crest, an emblem well known in the region and one that could strike a paralyzing fear into the hearts of those who inhabited it, for the crest identified its wearer as an agent of the cruel and merciless king who ruled with an unquestioned authority. Wherever His Royal Highness or his brutish emissaries roamed, a trail of anguish was sure to follow.

Still, the miller's daughter had always thought the punishments inflicted by the court were reserved for criminals, slackers, and insurgents. She never imagined it would sponsor the abduction and abuse of a virtuous young girl by two such wretched thugs. Of course she'd heard the stories of those who'd vanished from the town and were rumored to have been forced into an unholy service to their dark monarch. The wizened village elders who made a sport of such gossip often huddled in the church square to sneer and cluck and purse their lips over the fate of these "unfortunates cursed to become the unredeemable playthings of the king." But the miller's daughter was a hard-working, sensible child who dismissed these tales as nothing but the grim superstitions of some foolish old crones. She chose to believe instead that the missing were merely feisty youths who chafed under the rule of such a demanding despot and ran away of their own accord to seek their fortunes in a more hospitable clime.

Yet here they were, the king's men, with their cold hands and blank, black animal-hide faces, stealing her from the warmth and safety of her innocent bed and taking unspeakable liberties with her. Had she done something wrong? Was there some cause or provocation for this humiliation and debasement that she could not remember? And what did they mean by saying she was to become the king's property?

Before she could beg an explanation, the other fellow, the one who wasn't holding her in his indecorous grasp, slipped a queer sort of gag over her mouth, which silenced her utterly. It was an apparatus consisting of a series of leather straps fastened together into a sort of cage for the face and skull, similar to a dog's muzzle or a horse's harness, save for this one peculiar detail not found on an ordinary appliance meant to constrain the jaws of a rabid beast: a large, round, smooth leather ball was suspended in the center of the straps. This ball was inserted into the maiden's supple mouth, forcing her to stretch her jaws open to the extreme and contorting her lips into a vulnerable, gaping "O."

Thus trussed, the miller's daughter was forced to her knees with her shoulders and head bent to the floor and her buttocks raised high in the air. Her nightgown fell forward and settled around her in a lacy halo, rather prettily framing her spongy, red cunt and puckered asshole. These two openings shined dark against the lunar whiteness of her cheeks like a double bull's-eye.

"Your father says you can spin straw into gold, missy. That's quite a trick for a worthless whore. But if it's true, the king has decided to keep you as his slave. Of course, if it's a lie he will have you put to death."

"Now to be worthy of becoming a king's slave, you must be chaste in body and mind."

"Are you pure in both thought and deed? If you are you must certainly fear and loathe our treatment of you here tonight."

"If you are as good as the gold you spin, you must certainly wish for us to leave you unharmed and unbroken. And this fervent hope— that we not complete the delightful rape of your maidenhead—will leave your tender slit as dry as an autumn leaf."

"On the other hand, if you are really the slut we think you are, you will have a need for punishment and a secret desire to submit to our special brand of defilement."

With that, one of the men swiped a probing hand along the length of her splayed-open gash. She heard his mocking, muffled laughter as his hand came up just as coated with wetness as it would if she were being wooed by an adored lover.

"The gag may have silenced you, lady, but your lascivious nature speaks volumes. This pungent honey that flows from your virgin wound proves you are not fit for service to His Royal Highness as a cherished slave."

The miller's daughter wanted to object, she wanted desperately to be able to assert her purity and deny that she was stirred by the violence of the strangers, the harshness of the leather straps that crisscrossed her peachy cheeks, the threat (or promise?) of enslavement to a severe and punishing master. But in her heart she knew they were right; the body didn't lie. Perhaps this arousal could be taken as an admission of guilt and a sort of tacit consent to their cruel game.

So using only these copious juices and her silent, grateful tears for lubrication, the king's men took turns entering her again and again, enjoying the free use of her upturned backside, reveling in the pleasure her pain and degradation brought them all as they fucked her rosy bottom, but always being careful to preserve her womb's virginity for deflowerment by the all-mighty king.

———

In the morning the miller's daughter was brought to a tiny dungeon in the castle that contained a spinning wheel and stack upon stack of pungent straw. The only other furnishings in this grim chamber were a medieval set of shackles attached to the wall—ankle cuffs, wrist manacles, a collar to encircle her long, reedy neck, even a pair of heavy nipple clamps to hold her unruly bosom in check—and a hard wooden church pew provided for brief periods of rest and self-reflection.

She was stripped of her clothes, seated at the wheel, and hooked up to the collection of ancient irons. Now she was a study in contrasts: a soft, round, pink defenseless thing, as naked and mortal as a newborn baby, yet at the same time "dressed," outfitted at the extreme points of her person—the hands and feet, the tips of her breasts, the leather-gagged head—by hard, unyielding bonds of iron and chain, leashes to rein in and discipline an untrained dog.

"Spin, miller's harlot. Spin your straw into gold."

And with a final sardonic laugh they were gone. The prisoner heard the ringing "clink" of a padlock, and then she was alone in her disgrace, able to feel its sting even more sharply than when they'd kept her busy satisfying their lurid needs. How could this have happened to her, a poor, innocent child who had never known a moment's wrongdoing? But perhaps she was not as innocent as she liked to believe—there was, after all, the hot, moist evidence of her clandestine voluptuousness oozing forth from between her legs. So is that what it came to now? Was she to be punished for her unspoken cravings? Did she deserve to have been used in such a vulgar manner by these nameless, faceless apes under the banner of the king? To be stripped of her clothing along with her dignity and chained like a common mongrel in a yard? To be gagged and imprisoned, so she could not cry out and had to suffer in quiescent silence, accepting their rude violations with no hope of escape? She could barely sit at the spinning wheel, so injured and sore were her lower parts from the ungodly activities of the night before. And now she was expected to spin all this straw into gold or else she would be put to death! Of course she knew nothing of such alchemy—her father had simply been bragging to earn favor with the king so as to protect the family from the wrath of the court. But the miller's daughter had no choice. She had to try to work the magic her lord and master desired.

With a prayer in her heart she lifted a handful of straw to the spindle and began to work the wheel's pedal. The dull "clang" of iron rang out as her terrible manacles collided against each other. The weight of the clamps on her nipples, pulling as they did against the delicate flesh of her swaying breasts, made each congested tip darken and throb. Minutes turned into hours as the unhappy vassal spun and spun and spun. But, alas, there was no gold. Eventually, spent with her efforts, she collapsed upon the wooden pallet and slipped into a dreamless sleep that was as black and glassy as a puddle of ink.

———

This time the miller's daughter was awakened not by the two giant henchmen, but by a strange little man who held a bundle of birch rods tied together into a fearsome switch. As he barked at her, he cut the air with great swoops of the switch like he was wielding a sword against some invisible enemy.

"Wench!" cried the fellow. "You have displeased the king! You spin and spin, but there is no gold!"

The miller's daughter could not answer, gagged and bound as she was. But she searched the man's attire for the royal crest and nowhere could she find it. If he was not an official emissary of the king, how did he gain entrance to her cell? And what was his interest in her lot?

"Now you are doomed to die. But before the king puts his chattel to death he first extracts whatever pleasure he likes from their defenseless flanks. For instance, he might force you to swallow his bulging cock for breakfast every morning. Then again, he might simply whip you until he draws blood every night. Or perhaps he'll hand you over, like nothing but parcel of property, to his gang of depraved courtiers and instruct them to use you as they will. Then he'll simply sit back and watch you suffer while they bend you over and open you to their collective hands, tongues, and organs. This will be your final mortification before an untimely death."

Even with her secret longing to be owned and used thus by a strict, demanding master, the miller's daughter did not wish to die. The tiny man could see this when he peered into her eyes, the eyes of cornered prey, and he smiled a crooked smile.

"But I can save you, for I can spin straw into gold, and this very night I will turn that whole cartload of worthless hay into a king's ransom before the first light of dawn! I ask only two things in exchange for my services. First, you must allow me to punish you for your sins and insufficiencies. I would so enjoy administering proper corrective discipline to the shining buttocks of a worthless trollop like yourself."

So this was his gambit: He would replace the king's violence with his own! It was one thing to prostrate herself before a worthy master, to turn her whole being over to the lacerations of a king's whip because she was so lowly and he so grand, she so in need of moral and physical correction and he ordained by dint of his superiority, rank, and power to deliver her into that corrective state. But to simply be tortured by this dwarf, this birch-brandishing homunculus, for no purpose whatsoever except to bring him some sort of prurient pleasure—that was too much to bear! Still, she had no choice. To refuse him was to die. With a heavy heart, she nodded her consent.

"Excellent. Now, for the second part of our little bargain: If, because of my efforts at the spinning wheel, the king decides to make you his wife, you must agree to give me your first-born child."

To this the miller's daughter easily agreed, for what were the chances an exalted king would marry a common thing like herself? Especially as it had now been revealed that beneath her maidenly airs she harbored a lewd and shameful nature. If she was not pure enough to serve him as slave, surely she was not worthy to serve him as wife! This part of the contract she was sure would never be enforced, and so again she nodded consent.

Eager to extract his pleasure from the first half of the deal, the little manikin set about positioning his victim in the ideal posture for her punishment. He turned her to face the wall and tightened the chains on her wrists and ankles so she was stretched akimbo against the cold flagstones. Her leather-clad face and beleaguered nipples were pressed into the mossy chinks of the wall while her back and buttocks and plump thighs were unabashedly displayed to the lecherous eyes of her torturer.

When he was satisfied that her position would afford him the maximum access in this delightful beating, he took his place behind her and lifted his bundle of sticks (which he refered to as his "training rod") high over his head, then brought it down, hard, against her unblemished rear. The sounds this made—a high-pitched siren of a whistle then the "thwack" as twigs met flesh, leaving both the rod and the receiver marked as they'd not been before—grew into a strange kind of music as he played his instrument against her in a rhythmic assault. Slowly at first, and then faster and faster, his training rod sang its song on her hips, buttocks, and thighs, and the player punctuated each stroke of the baton with a chanted slur against the wayward maid.

Hiss/thwack, "Slut!" Hiss/smack, "Whore!" Hiss/crack, "Liar and infidel! Your father promised gold, but did you deliver? Of course not! Liars and children of liars must be taught a lesson!" Hiss/thwack, hiss/smack, the birch branches cut into her again and again, leaving great, red welts in their wake, making the poor maiden writhe against her iron bonds as she twisted this way and that trying in vain to avoid the agonizing blows. Alas, there was no escaping the relentless fall of the rod. From behind her leather gag she uttered guttural moans and stifled screams. Boiling tears spilled from her panicked eyes and soaked the leather straps that bound her face. Tiny droplets of blood, like ruby chips, dotted the welts and gashes that the crazed martinet inflicted on her hind parts. But still he would not let up.

"Strumpet!" Swoosh. "Useless cow!" Thwack. "Well, now you must bow to me, mustn't you? Now you must grovel and fawn and submit to my will if you wish to see tomorrow!"

His raspy voice rose and rose with furious excitement as he laid ever more crimson stripes upon the milk-white flesh, and just as the unhappy girl fainted dead away from the acute sensations of pleasure and pain, the little man erupted in an enormous gushing orgasm all over her well-seasoned globes.

———

Some time later the miller's daughter awoke to find herself alone. She was still chained and gagged, still naked and trembling, but now somehow less naked, as her derriere from the small of her back to the bend of her knees was dressed in a lattice of blisters and cuts. Purple welts and pink gashes were woven together like a fine lace petticoat and spread across her back and thighs in a veil of pain, and the only available balm to cool this burning garment was her tormentor's sticky effusion, which he'd left exactly where it fell, in gobs of dripping wet ness, upon the sleeping beauty.

Fortunately, the little man had also left her spool after spool of gleaming spun gold in place of the straw. And the king was so pleased with these riches, which he assumed were the result of the maiden's handiwork, he decided to make her his wife!

———

Years passed, and the miller's daughter, despite her longing to be slave and not queen, accepted her lot with the grace of unquestioning obedience. She attended to her duties and comported herself with all the propriety befitting her newly exalted station. But she was restless and unfulfilled, for despite his reputation, she found her husband's appetite, at least insofar as it applied to her, rather pallid. He rarely came to her bed except to conceive an heir. And while a tour of the castle revealed that the private halls and chambers were outfitted with a variety of indecent devices—whips and harnesses and complicated rigs for flogging—the fixtures in the queen's suite were as comfortable and ordinary as those in a picture book.

It seemed the king regarded marriage as sacred and therefore not in the least bit sensual, reserving gratification of his more piquant tastes for the legendary lost ones of the village, the legion of silent slaves who padded naked and barefoot through the lower depths of the castle wearing the same irons and gags and nipple clamps that had once adorned the miller's daughter, carrying out the grunt work of the household by day while satisfying the proclivities of their exacting king by night.

Because the last time she was allowed to venture into the cavernous underworld beneath the castle was when she'd been locked away in the dungeon to spin, the queen never actually laid eyes on these shadow slaves. But her ears confirmed their existence when, in the depth of her loneliest nights, she heard their far-off cries of anguish uniting with the climactic screams of her lord and master as he used their bound, prone, and tortured bodies to absorb his passion and his rage over and over again. During these times she would recall the details of her own voluptuous episode in the dungeon when the strange little man had flagellated her naked rump so thoroughly her filthy secrets were purified. She remembered how he had lashed her like she was a misbehaving colt and he a severe jockey bent on training her wayward hindparts with his birchwood crop until she begged and pleaded for mercy and finally passed out from the force of her hunger for such a beating. She remembered, as she rolled herself between furious fingers until the soapy wet bubble of her lust expanded and popped between her legs, the whistle of his rod as it split the air. She remembered the crack as it landed, the burn like a cattle brand on her great hams as wood bit into skin, the taste of the leather in her mouth, and the humiliation in her excited gut. But what she never remembered, because it had seemed so far off and preposterous, was the devil's contract she'd entered into with her harsh instructor. So it came as a cruel shock when, after the birth of her first child, the little man showed up for his due.

"I come for the child," he said blandly, as if it were commonplace to take a babe from its mother's breast.

"No, please, I beg of you," said the queen. "I'll give you anything else you ask, but not my child!"

"What have you that I could possibly want?"

"Why, I have everything! I am the king's wife and all the riches of the kingdom are at my disposal."

"Aye, you are indeed the king's wife, but you only achieved that lofty station because I spun spool after spool of straw into gold! So you must realize that riches of that sort are nothing to me; I can simply spin them whenever I want. No, Your Highness, the only way I shall grant you clemency in this bargain is if you can guess my name. I'll give you three chances, and if you can't call me by my proper name, the child is mine."

"Is it Balthazar?" asked the queen.

"No," he replied.

"Is it Alouisious?"

"Wrong again!"

"Is it...Rumpelstiltskin!?"

The little man searched the eyes of the beautiful queen and there he found the same craving for correction that he had seen there when she was nothing but a doomed miller's daughter. With a twist of his gargoyle lips, he chuckled softly before he pronounced his answer.

"No, slut. No, Rumpelstiltskin is not my name!"

"Wait!" implored the queen, "I think I know. It is...Master," she whispered as she sank to the floor before the knave and threw her skirts up over her head. Her exposed buttocks quivered and quaked in happy anticipation of the cruel lashing it had needed for so long.

"Yes! Master!" cried the little man, and the air rang out with the song of his rod as it came crashing down on the waiting, willing target groveling at his feet.

The End

The Sleeping Beauty

Once upon a time…

…the question was posed: What's in a kiss? Not just any kiss, but that particular kiss that awakens the sleeping beauty in lovers. It should be simple to answer; a kiss is, after all, just lip upon lip, tongue wrapped around tongue in an embrace like the coiled necks of mating doves, or the gesture of unity between two entwined pinkies to say, "Yes, I am with you." But that is only the physical description—lip to lip, tongue to tongue, hot breath, the private pocket of humidity formed when two searching mouths come so close—and there is so much more than the physical to this act, is there not? For between the lips of lovers entire souls can pass. As one exhales, she releases herself and the other catches it up in his inward breath, ingesting her very essence into his own. In this way selves are exchanged, again and again and again, until a boundary-less blending occurs.

And so it was with that gifted beauty of legend, Aurora, whose very existence on this earth hinged on the magic of a kiss….

Despite attempts in every manner and position, her parents could not conceive a child. They longed to share their lives with a son or daughter, but they were barren for so long that they began to lose hope. Without the promise of a joyful procreation, their lovemaking began to slowly disintegrate, turning from a mutually satisfying union into a sordid, disconnected act of selfish lust. He would wake with a raging erection, its angry, purple-headed shaft leaping and writhing under the pressure of engorgement like an electric eel searching for prey. She would refuse him entry, teasing him mercilessly as she mauled and fingered her pointed, burning clit to a violent orgasm right in front of his eyes. Then, only after she'd finished herself off with this one-sided climax, would she soften enough to allow him to take his own pleasure between her thighs. Now all slick and buttered up with the juices of self-gratification, she would turn her back to him and let her legs fall open. Her rounded buttocks lay before him like a decadent satin cushion and the wet portal just below showed its satin lining like a red flag to a bull. With one hand he scooped her up under her belly and raised her pelvis to just the right angle. With his other hand he pressed open her still-swollen vaginal lips and then plunged the full length of himself between her slackened muscles. Thus, uttering the grunts and howls of a mad dog, he would take his wife again and again until he drove it home to the explosive final thrust. But even though he was buried deep inside her, it was as if he were all alone. He poured his musk and cream all the way up her, almost to her heart, but since this liquid offering didn't seem to be able to give her the child she longed for, she ignored the gift, lying with her face down in the pillows, slipping away into her self-induced afterglow, and receiving her husband's amorous assaults with a detachment that bordered on disdain. And, above all, they never kissed.

———

Then one day, while bathing in the stream, a horned toad hopped upon the woman's naked belly. She screamed with disgust and brushed it off in a panic, but later that night a strange sort of toad-man visited her in a dream.

"Madame," said the creature. "Do not fear me. I come with good tidings. You long for a child, do you not? Heed my advice and you shall have your dear babe. In the morning, when your husband wishes to make love to you, do not stave him off in your usual manner or turn your back on his desires. Make love as you used to, with mutual exultation and reciprocity, and at the moment of complete convergence, kiss each other. Insert your tongue deep within your husband's hungry mouth, let him suck gently upon your lower lip, inhale his breath as he devours you, exhale your essence into his heart, lungs, and belly, and you shall conceive the most beautiful baby girl in the world."

The woman followed the toad's instructions, and sure enough, nine months later, the couple had their hoped-for child. They named her Aurora and held a magnificent party to celebrate her birth. Among the invited guests were twelve accomplished oracles who read the spiritual secrets of the babe and predicted her auspicious future. The first saw lifelong health for the young maid. The second predicted incomparable grace and wit. The third felt sure she would never want for money or material possessions. And on they went, prophesizing a charmed future of happiness, extreme beauty, and goodwill for little Aurora.

But before the twelfth oracle could confer her prediction upon the child, a furious old woman crashed the party, looking like a demon and screaming about how she, too, was a seer of souls, and why wasn't she invited to celebrate along with the others? The truth was, the happy couple, in the excitement and confusion of the whole affair, had simply forgotten to invite this thirteenth oracle. Now she was insulted, and in her outrage she cursed the tiny lass with an evil prediction for the future: "When she reaches the age of consent her innocence shall be pricked and she shall bleed to death before tasting the fullness of womanhood!"

Aurora's parents were heartbroken. Could it be their lovely daughter would not live past her chaste adolescence? Just then, the twelfth oracle, who had not yet shared her omen, stepped up to the bassinet where the infant lay.

"I cannot completely dispel the prediction of the thirteenth oracle," she told them. "But I can soften the blow by telling you what I see in Aurora's future. She will indeed be pricked by the arrow of an unworthy suitor. But she will not die! Instead, she will fall into a deep, unconscious slumber and nothing but the most passionate kiss of tenderness shall awaken her to the full joys of womanhood."

Aurora's mother was relieved to know that at least her child would not perish prematurely, but would only sleep in the dusk of a nether world. Still, her father could not bear to think of his darling girl losing her consciousness in such a manner, and he vowed to keep from her any who might pierce her innocence. He built a massive fortress and confined his family to its inner bowels. The food, entertainment, and education were provided by elderly gentlewomen, and under no circumstances were any men permitted to cross the threshold for fear of meeting the wrath of the protective patriarch.

Then, on the eve of her eighteenth birthday, Aurora began to feel a strange discontent. For all these years she had never questioned the sanctity of her home or her way of life, but now she wondered if perhaps there was something beyond the fortress walls, something out there in the world that her dear father so assiduously shunned, that might be worth discovering. She decided it was time to venture forth despite her parents' warnings about the horrors that awaited beyond their cozy stronghold. She began to scour the castle in the hopes of finding some unsecured chink or forgotten tunnel that might open her way to freedom, and while on the hunt for such a place, she wandered into a forgotten room at the top of a tower.

Opening the door (one of the only unlatched portals she had ever encountered), Aurora entered a windowless, unlit room and gingerly felt her way in the pressing darkness. Suddenly she lost her balance, and flailing her arms in front of her to break the fall, she expected to hit the dusty floor with her outstretched hands. But instead her palms landed on the heaving torso of an unknown man. She couldn't see his face in the blackness that surrounded them but she could feel his acid breath burn her cheeks as a pair of muscular arms pulled her close. She would have screamed, she should have screamed in shock and fear, but her curiosity quickly overtook the impulse. She did, however, gasp with surprise and a kind of aroused verve, for until now she'd never felt the embrace of any man except her flaccid, aged father and she'd never smelled the heady musk a young man exudes when he's full of longing, need, and fire. There, in the protective cloak of darkness, she was pinned against a hard, naked chest unadorned by the smooth curve of a woman's breast but wild with a mat of woolly hair that tickled her nostrils and irritated her cheek, and the newness of these sensations excited and seduced her into a willing acquiescence. Aurora opened her mouth to receive the lips and tongue of her mysterious stranger, thinking that this first kiss would begin a languorous journey into the whole array of sensual delights.

But he eschewed her offered lips, and without her desired kiss to soften the way, he kicked apart her legs, ripped off her panties, and impaled her upon his pointed prick. Now the scream she'd failed to let forth before broke from her open mouth and curdled the blood that flowed. But she did not feel the pain for more than an instant, for all at once she fell into a deep sleep, just as the twelfth oracle had predicted.

An eternity passed, and the sleeping beauty lay in the same stillness that had overtaken her at the moment of her deflowering. Nobody, not even her loving parents, could awaken her. It was as if she was waiting in a state of suspended animation for the special kiss the seer said would break these bonds and restore her to a full life.

Then one night, when the rest of the world was asleep, a young prince found his way to the tower room where Aurora slept. He had heard many stories about the maid who lay in wait for her true love's special kiss to enliven her, but he also heard that numerous men had tried, to no avail—all their best efforts fell on lips as pale and cold as moon stone. Still, he felt he had to attempt to wake the angel whose first taste of love had turned so bitter.

As he crept into Aurora's chamber, he carried a scented candle that cast just enough light for him to see the face and form of the dreamless one, and now it was his turn to gasp; her high cheekbones, elegant chin, flawless complexion, and ripe lips so surpassed the usual description of beauty that it almost made him ache. Her youthful figure, forever preserved in its slumbering state, showed long legs, a tiny waist, soft shoulders, and the firm fleshy mounds of perfect, untouched breasts that seemed to invite the onlooker to handle them with abandon.

The prince set down his candle and leaned over to kiss the vulnerable, bloodless lips that lay before him. But just before his mouth met hers, he stopped, deciding on another approach entirely. He moved down to where her dainty feet lay motionless and slid them up, up, up, bending her knees until they fell open, exposing the full view of her other lips. Then he crawled between these unguarded thighs and brought his face way up close to her velvet slit until he could smell the delicate, briny perfume from within. He parted the brier patch of pubic hair and then slowly, ever so slowly, he reached out his tongue and traced the edges of flesh with its wet tip. Moving in even closer, he began to gently nibble on the reddened lips, feeling them plump in his mouth as he sucked and suckled. Soon he moved to the pink nub of her clitoris, using his tongue to alternately encircle it with its tip, then press and release against it with the wider center, until it grew from a tiny closed rosebud to a blooming, pulsating trunk. Dew began to stream from her, moistening the entire length of her engorged organ and covering the prince's nose, mouth, and chin with a slick, salt-sweet coating. On and on he went, kissing, licking, sucking, and nibbling, feeling the heat gather in her juicy parts until the whole region seemed to be quivering with liquid incandescence. Finally, when he felt her very close to the edge, he sunk his long tongue deep within her scooped out vagina and pressed his upper lip and teeth against her throbbing, raging clit. He exhaled his soul into her opening, she ingested it through her very center, and returned his love by sending out her soul in wave after wave of orgasm, and with the rhythmic flow of these intense contractions, her entire face transformed—her eyes flew open, her throat and mouth and tongue uttered guttural moans, her head rolled side to side in vibrant ecstasy, and at last, from receiving this most passionate and tender kind of kiss, the sleeping beauty came fully alive.

The End

The Three Little Pigs

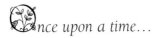*nce upon a time…*

…there was a refrain chanted by smart-mouthed little girls to taunt and tease any boy who might be slovenly, rambunctious, or otherwise badly behaved. "Who's afraid of the big bad wolf, the big bad wolf, the big bad wolf?" the girls would sing, and then they'd throw themselves, limbs akimbo, upon the offender. Shiny patent leather Mary Janes would dig into his groin as long hair flayed out in a web of static electricity. White cotton underpants with cornrows of lace or the days of the week embroidered upon the seat would be flown like a victor's flag and the ravenous little she-wolf would pin her prey to the ground and pretend to eat him all up, "mmmm mmmm good, yummy in my tummy."

It may seem strange for the girl to be the aggressor, tackling the hapless fellow in a cascade of giggles. But as often as not the female of such an age is bigger and better coordinated than her male counterpart, and during this unique time in her development may enjoy a dominance over her quarry that she'll never experience as a fully grown adult. Unless, that is, she is still forced to assert this big bad part of herself because some little boys simply refuse to grow up….

In the small town of Hoggs Corners, tucked away far from civilization on the ridge of a remote cluster of impenetrable mountains, lived three men. While quite different from one another in physique, lifestyle, and personality, they were very close friends who were brought together by the fact that they shared one overriding trait: Each one behaved like a naughty little piglet and each one was very much in need of a she-wolf's corrective instruction.

The first man, Mister Hayman, suffered from one of the deadliest sins: He was slovenly beyond compare. His sink contained unwashed dishes dating back years, his bed was nothing but a pile of straw with a filthy rucksack tossed upon it, his floors were so covered with soil and dust that they appeared to be the dirt floors of a rustic cottage even though underneath was a layer of shoddy linoleum. Hayman was incomparably lazy, refusing to work or do any physical activity, and so he mostly just sat around the shack all day long drinking beer and eating cold, greasy hash straight out of an encrusted kettle. He had no friends or social life, had never had a lady friend (what woman would venture into such a pit?), and was so indolent and reclusive that he rarely even got dressed in the morning, preferring to lie about naked, scratching his belly and playing with his greasy penis in the privacy of his own mess. Over the years this sedentary lifestyle caused him to balloon up into a ludicrous sort of corpulence complete with puffy calves, a fleshy chest, and two gigantic porkchops for hind quarters. But even though he was a big fat pig whose pectorals were so flabby he almost looked womanly, his maleness was clearly established by his possession of a big fat penis, which he employed in frequent bouts of self-gratification.

Just down the road from Hayman's sty lived the second fellow, Mister Woodman. Unlike his corpulent young neighbor, Woodman was an older man who was slender to the point of being slight, with long, tapered fingers and a dick like a paring knife. He also differed from Hayman in that he kept his house beautifully and filled his home with alluring things—divans covered in animal skins, vases filled with exotic orchids or bouquets of rare feathers, music boxes that played hypnotic tunes, and hampers filled with a luscious variety of rich foods and intoxicating drink in every room. But like Hayman, Woodman could also be called a pig because of his incorrigible womanizing. His opulent, excessive, sensual lifestyle was intended to lure a limitless parade of young women into his bed, and not in the manner of the so-called "serial monogamist" in which the lover is at least faithful to one woman at a time. No, Woodman's game was to romance several women at once, on the sly and behind their backs, betraying them all and breaking each and every heart. No matter how much he claimed to want to someday settle down and be faithful to "the right woman," he continued to gorge himself upon a feast of female flesh, with no regard for the women as he racked up an endless string of conquests like so many links in a sausage.

Finally, just across the way from Woodman, resided Mister Brickman, the alpha-swine among the brood. Unlike his two cohorts, Brickman's boarishness could not be found in the fact that he was too sloppy or too fat or too onanistic or too rapacious. In fact, Brickman was the ideal man—handsome, sexy, smart, witty, kind, generous, talented, caring, dependable, passionate, well-endowed, wealthy, and single. But "single" does not necessarily connote "available." Where Hayman and Woodman would have liked to find mates if their bad habits hadn't precluded it, Brickman, despite being perfect marriage material, was happily and contentedly committed to remaining uncommitted, safe, and invulnerable behind a wall of bachelorhood. Which, in the minds of a number of women, made him the biggest pig of all.

———

One day, when they least expected it, these three porcine pals were visited by a certain Miss Canidae Wolfe—known simply as "Candy"— who turned out to be another kind of animal altogether. Statuesque and voluptuous, with a feral gleam in her eye and a scent about her like a beast in heat, Candy was unlike any woman the men had known (or, in Hayman's case, imagined). Her beauty was extreme and frightening; her age was impossible to determine because while she had a face as ruddy and unlined as a newborn's it was crowned by an anachronism of silver-white hair that frizzed out in a furry halo about her head. She also declined to shave the soft sterling down that covered her legs and sprouted from her fragrant underarms and this made her seem even more like an untamed creature reveling in its bestiality. But the most striking thing about Candy's appearance had to be her outrageous mouth: A pair of oversized lips, always moist like a canine's chops, curled easily into a crafty smile and then, in a light-ning flash, would suddenly pucker up in a mocking pout that could elicit a dizzying breathlessness in even the most stoical of men. If she was aroused her long, wet tongue would slither out of her mouth with remarkable agility and finesse from between a set of the most stunning white fangs. And it seemed she could almost dislodge her jaw from its hinges, much as a snake does, allowing objects of massive proportion to slide easily into her hungry maw.

This fabulous predator arrived first at Hayman's house.

"Knock, knock, Mr. Hayman!" she cried.

"What do you want?" squeaked the little porker within.

"Why, to eat you, of course!"

"No, no! Not by the hairs on my chinny chin chin!"

But it was not the hairs on his chinny chin chin that she was confronted with when she pushed against the corroded doorframe and forced her way into the house. It was an entirely other set of hairs that met her gaze, the proverbial "short hairs" that sprouted around the thick, bald joint of meat that was Hayman's much-abused organ and which he was once again cradling and worrying in his busy little paws.

"You are disgusting," she drawled. "Just look at you! You lie amid this squalor with nothing better to do than tug at your pathetic cock all day long! Stop playing with yourself and clean this place up, little piggy, or pay the price!"

But Hayman was simply incapable of changing his dirty ways and Candy had no choice but to teach him a lesson. In a trice, she had him hogtied and naked, kneeling on his fat haunches and begging for mercy. But no lenience could be shown to such a grotesque violator of all that is clean and decent. He had to be punished, and punished well. She began with an open-handed spanking of his naked, blubbery hams, slapping the slabs of white meat like they were less-than-prime cuts in need of tenderizing.

"Filthy pig!" she shouted with each resounding smack. "Let me hear you cry 'oinkle!' "

"No, stop, please!" cried the unfortunate Hayman, but he was powerless against his foe. Large, glutinous tears dropped from his beady eyes as a crimson flush of pain and shame spread over his quivering globes, but nothing could sway the lady butcher from her self-appointed task of curing his meat until his rump was well roasted. Finally, when she was convinced that his hide was properly tanned, she stopped to catch her breath.

"Please," the chubby little shoat whined. "Untie me, I beg of you!"

"Not until you cry 'oinkle!' Until then, you'll have to bear the pain. Unless living a life of shiftless self-indulgence made you too soft to take a little pain, pig boy."

But when Hayman moaned and rolled over on his fat back, trussed up arms and legs sticking straight into the air like a slaughtered wildebeest, Candy saw that it was not the pain of the spanking that was vexing him as much as the queer ache from a mighty case of blue balls. His penis, as broad and blunt as a bludgeoning shillelagh, was fully erect. It stood out from the folds of his fluffy belly like a shiny, hard goat horn in the midst of a flock of lambs. His giant testicles had tightened into an enraged fist, and the whole affair—cock and balls alike—was vibrating with an anticipation that made it seem separate from the rest of his person, an independent critter writhing with unfulfilled needs, stuck like a powerful but tottering phallic root into the mushy quicksand of his groin, defying gravity and the laws of physics to rise monumental above the bog. The air around this tremulous organ seemed to shimmer the way the atmosphere of a desert landscape does in a heat wave, distorting one's vision and making it seem even more autonomous from its owner, more alive, more keenly sensitive, more tortured.

"Aha. I see," murmured Candy through her drooling smile. "That's why you want me to untie your hands, isn't it? So you can beat your juicy sausage to a pulp, like you usually do. But it's time to grow up, pig boy, time to wean you off of playing with yourself and introduce you to the way the big boars play!

With that, the long-legged she-beast stood over her kill and exposed her glistening cunt to his view. Slowly she lowered herself into the heat-infused ambiance around his dick, lowered herself gingerly onto this rotisserie spit, seared her tender cut with its blazing fire while his cool, flabby torso cushioned her gyrating ass. She could barely straddle the entire breadth of him, but once she was settled in the saddle it was a very comfortable ride indeed. She rode and rode like a stuck pig, bouncing up and down on his curly tail, grabbing handfuls of his fleshy midriff to use as reins while she steadied herself for the shattering climax. She felt the delightful opposites of his burning volcanic rock penis on her insides and the cool, shifting sands of his ample belly sloshing beneath her. She wouldn't let him come, the avaricious Miss Candy Wolfe, but she came all over him, basting his ham hocks until the juices ran clear. Then she quickly rolled off her perch.

"Nooooo," cried the frustrated shoat, whose testes were bluer than ever, "No, no, n-o-o-o-o-!"

"Aw, what's the matter my little weanling? I won't leave you all greased up with nowhere to slide, I promise! But I wouldn't want you to impregnate me with a litter of little piglets, now would I? They'd all be lazy, worthless slovenly sloths, just like their fat, filthy sire! No, no, instead of letting you come inside me, little piggy, I'll huff and I'll puff and I'll blow you down!"

She crawled upon his massive chest and unhinged her acrobatic jaw. Then she swallowed down his purple meat in one delicious gulp. As he spewed himself into her throat, he squealed with unmatched delight.

"Oink, oink...oinkle!"

"You see?" she chortled as she swallowed his cum. "This way there's no sticky mess to clean up."

And from that day forward, Hayman became an impeccable house-keeper whose cleanliness was so pleasing to women they nearly always agreed to help him avoid a sticky mess in just this manner.

Next the wolverina visited Woodman's pleasure palace. Of course entering his abode proved no problem whatsoever, as the insatiable hog could never turn a beautiful female away from his door.

"Knock, knock, Mr. Woodman!" she murmured through the keyhole in her most seductive growl. He welcomed the exquisite beast into his inner sanctum with an elegant flourish.

"Come in, come in. What can I do for you, my pretty young thing?"

"Why, I want nothing more than to eat you, kind sir!"

"How delightful," he grunted, and he stripped down to his naked hide. "Enjoy your feast, and do not quit until you reach the hairs on my chinny chin chin!"

But Candy's plan was not to simply indulge this faithless fellow in his selfish pleasure. He needed to pay for his pig-like behavior toward women, and to this end she whipped out her trusty ropes and informed him that he was to be hogtied before being led to delightful slaughter. Accustomed as he was to the gratification of all sorts of sexual urges in all sorts of women, Woodman assumed this was simply a harmless proclivity that amused the lady, so he offered no resistance. He chuckled good naturedly and held his wrists out in front of him to receive the rough twine bindings. But to his surprise, Candy did not proceed with the shackling.

"It's not that simple, pig. I have no beef with your romantic history, but there are many others who would love to rub your snout in it, so to speak. To this end, I shall cover you in viscous lard and set these other she-wolves upon you and the first one to pin you down will be the lucky lady who gets to bind you up and lead you to market. Then all the others will take a piece of you until you are nothing but a well-chewed spare rib. Only after we have made you cry 'oinkle' will you be a reformed little piggy who goes 'wee wee wee' all the way home and never strays from his lady love."

In an instant she poured a slop bucket of grease over his head and swung open the back door of his cottage. There stood an army of women whom Woodman had wronged in the past. They were fully naked but their bodies were painted and feathered like a tribe of island warriors, making them seem clothed and invulnerable and making Woodman's clean pink and white flesh somehow even more naked by comparison. When the ladies saw the object of their rage standing there so humiliated and exposed, covered with bacon grease and wearing a shocked expression on his usually impassive face, they whooped and hollered and charged into the house to surround their cornered quarry. One after another of these past lovers—formerly nice girls who were now transformed into vengeful savages—threw themselves upon the greased pig and tried to wrestle him to the floor. Time and again he slithered through their grasps and skittered away, only to be pounced on by the next set of flailing arms, suffocating bosoms, vise-like thighs. But even though he feared their wrath, were one of them to finally pin him down, he also couldn't help becoming pitifully aroused. His long, pointed penis, usually as straight as a spear, began to twist into an engorged corkscrew like a piggy's tail. He ached to plunge this throbbing helix into each of the sweet troughs that surrounded him, to feel the envelopes of moist flesh close over his cock as it spiraled deep into these wells. He began to enjoy being tackled over and over again, for each time he would writhe and wiggle in just such a way as to surreptitiously slip his well-greased dipstick into the attacker's slit. The woman would shriek when she felt him thrust, shriek and throw her hands in the air and thus completely lose any advantage she'd gained over the little beast so that he'd ooze right out of her and slither away until the next wrangler leaped upon his haunches.

Finally one gal was able to keep the squealing swine in her clutches long enough to slip the ropes around his flailing limbs until he was properly subdued. His crazy cock was nearly spinning off its moorings on his hoary belly, so desperate was he to come. But true to her word, Miss Canidae Wolfe would not grant him satisfaction until his captor and her compatriots had received restitution for their past sufferings. Tied up and powerless, he was forced to fully satisfy each of the tribal hunters who had brought him to this ritual slaying of his pork-barrel ego. But he himself was not allowed to climax upon threat of becoming the subject of an actual slaying.

When all the women had finally had their fill, Candy agreed to relieve the poor man.

"Now I will huff and puff and blow you down," she sang. And in one gulp, she sucked him into her magical mouth.

"Oink, oink…oinkle!" Woodman squealed as he exploded all over her dripping fangs.

"Very good, piggy. You have acquiesced. And if you promise to settle down and remain faithful to whomever you are dating at any particular time, if you promise to be a very good boy who always brings home the bacon and fries it up in the pan, then you shall be allowed to snort for this sort of tasty truffle with your special lady whenever you like."

From that day forward, Woodman stopped womanizing and lying and cheating and began treating his girlfriends with the utmost respect. He never saw more than one woman at a time and he only moved on to the next when it was mutually agreed that the relationship had come to an end. And, needless to say, women simply ate him up.

But Brickman. Ah, Brickman, he was a problem. For no matter how hard she huffed and puffed and blew him down, Miss Canidae Wolfe could not change this uber pig perennial bachelor into a domesticated husband.

And then one day something happened. Instead of her huffing and puffing and blowing him down, she turned the tables on him and made him blow her down. As his hungry mouth and slippery tongue flicked and flacked and sucked and smacked at her boiling kettle, she reached down and grabbed him by the hairs on his chinny chin chin and screamed, "Oinkle!" until the pigs came home.

Brickman knew he had finally met his match, and asked Miss Canidae Wolfe if she would do him the honor of becoming Mrs. Canidae Wolfe-Brickman. And from that day forward they lived happily ever after.

The End

Hansel and Gretel

O̶nce upon a time…

…when great famine was upon the land, a brother and sister were led into the forest and abandoned by their father and stepmother so the beleaguered family would have fewer mouths to feed. Or so the tale went, until these secret diaries were discovered….

———

GRETEL:
The night we were disowned was the night of my first serious date. Sure, I'd hung around with guys in a group situation, but never just one-on-one with someone who had asked me out. It meant a lot to me—I really wanted it to work out, really wanted a boyfriend. See, ever since my father married my stepmother—who, of course, was the typical evil stepmother who hated the children of her husband's first wife and was jealous of any attention he gave us—we kids had been literally starved for affection. I didn't know if it affected Hansel so much; he was a guy and kind of hard to figure out since he usually kept up that dumb "strong, silent type" attitude. But I knew if I didn't experience some attention and kindness from someone soon, I

would waste away like one of those waifs in the fairy tales.

So I took a whole lot of care dressing for this date, trying on first one skirt then another until I found the perfect outfit. After each costume change I paraded in front of Hansel, pretending I was a glamorous fashion model, turning and posing and cocking my leg just so to better display a jutting hip bone or an elegant calf.

"Do you like this one?"

"I guess," he growled. "Whatever."

Hansel lay on his unmade bed in a pair of jeans and a white T-shirt that smelled pleasing and powdery like laundry detergent and stretched tight across his muscular arms and chest like a second skin. I wished the guy I was dating was built like that, but no, those beautiful biceps and shoulders had to be wasted on my brother. Anyway, Hansel pretended not to be that interested in my fashion dilemma, but I noticed he never got up off the bed to flick on one of his video games or play his music. He just peered up at my "silly" display from beneath half-shut, heavy-lidded eyes. And he kept shaking his foot in that fast, rhythmic way he did whenever he was nervous or excited.

HANSEL:

My sister Gretel is the one who got us thrown out, I guess. Whatever. See, she was going out with some moron from school—a real Neanderthal who didn't deserve to lick the ground a girl like Gretel walked on, much less take her on a date—and she kept insisting I help pick out what she wore. Like any guy really cares what a girl wears. All these horn dogs want to know about a girl's clothing is how quickly it can come off, you know? But it seemed important to her.

She kept coming back into my room in different skirts, and each time they got shorter and shorter, showing off more and more of her legs. Gretel has really long legs. I mean really long. And smooth. I guess she shaves them or something like that, but I've never really seen legs so smooth before. I knew I wasn't supposed to notice that, but hey, she kept strutting and posing like some kind of stupid fashion model or something, and you know how you can't really avoid their legs when they do that posing thing. I also know I was supposed to make her wear something that would say "good girl" to this idiot boyfriend she was going to see so he wouldn't get the wrong idea, but she kept saying she wanted it to be "a little bit saucy" because she really liked the guy and wanted it to work out. You know it hasn't exactly been fat city around here in the affection department ever since my dad married the wicked witch. It's been what you might call an emotional famine, and I knew Gretel was hungry for love. So I didn't really want to contribute to her starvation and I told her to wear the really short skirt. Like I said, she has really long legs.

GRETEL:
The thing about Hansel is he acts all distant and haughty, especially since our parents split up, but I know underneath that tough exterior he's really OK—he's just the same guy who used to wrestle with me and let me win when we were kids. Lots of times he would pin me down and sit on top of me while he held my arms against the floor above my head and laughed and laughed. I would struggle like mad, writhing and sweating and protesting until my hair was a total tangle and my skirt was all bunched up around my waist and my shirt but-

tons were ripped off and I was completely out of breath. Then he would get that same look in his eyes that he had the night of the date—that slitty-lidded, far away look—and he'd snap the elastic of my cotton panties, saying, "Gotcha." But he knew I hated to lose, and when he could see that I was really upset he'd suddenly weaken his grasp, allowing me to throw him off, flip him over, and overcome him, making me the victor and he the trapped prey.

"Damn, sis. You're just too strong for me," he would murmur, and as young and stupid as I was, I believed that I'd really gotten the upper hand. Then I would feel sorry for him and make him take off his shirt and lie on his belly so I could give him a back rub, which he always said I did better than anyone in the world.

Yeah, he's really a pretty good brother. Which was why I was surprised when he didn't try to stop me from wearing the leather micromini. I mean, I really expected him to get all protective and bossy on me and to tell me I had to wear the long, grey wool skirt or he'd tell Dad. But when I came out to model the short leather number, he just stared a little longer than usual and stopped shaking his foot.

"Your panties show."

"They do not!" I pulled the skirt down, but really, they didn't show.

"Do, too," he insisted. "Right here." He pulled me over to the bed and reached one hand up the back of my bare thigh to the rim of my panties. Then he snapped the elastic hard against my butt, just like he did when we were kids. Only now the panties were black lace bikinis instead of white cotton briefs.

"Ow!" I complained.

"Gotcha."

"Come on, Hansel. What do you think? Really."

"Wear that one."

"Yeah? It's not too short?"

"OK, you're right. Don't wear that one. I don't give a damn."

He swung his legs over the far edge of the bed and stood up, turning his back on the whole affair. "I'm busy," he mumbled, and grabbed his Strad. He began to furiously finger its slim neck like he was playing a bunch of fancy riffs, but he didn't turn on the amp.

"No, really, I need your opinion," I cooed.

"Why? What difference does it make?"

"You're a guy. You know what guys like."

He turned and looked at me again. I did my best, most model-y pose for him, hands on hips, leg turned out, spine slouched, and pelvis thrust forward almost in his face.

"Wear that one."

As I left the room I heard him turn on the amplifier and start to practice some chords, but he couldn't seem to hit the right notes.

HANSEL:

Gretel got back about midnight. I should've creamed her for being so late, especially since Dad and the witch were too self-involved to notice. But hey, it was her first serious date and like I said, it was important to her. So I thought I'd cut her a little slack. She came into my room without knocking, and I was lying on my bed almost naked except for my jockeys and my Strad, which was hanging low on the strap across my chest. This time I didn't really give her a hard time for forgetting to knock because she was crying.

"Bastard!" she spit. I didn't know if she meant me or Dad or the date guy or what, but something about it made me laugh. I mean, I know she was upset, but she looked kind of cute cursing like she was a goddamned sailor.

"What? Did he get fresh on you, sissy?" I hit a diminished seventh on the guitar for effect.

"Totally not! He didn't even try to kiss me."

See, I really hate to see Gretel cry. It really bums me out. I wasn't sure what to do. Then I thought of something.

"Wanna wrestle?"

"What?" Maybe it was stupid, but she did stop crying.

"Bet you can't beat me."

"Bet I can," she laughed, and in an instant she was on me. Of course she was like a thin little noodle next to me—a really soft, smooth noodle—and I had her flat on her back in an instant. Usually at this point I feel sorry for her and let her throw me. But that night I just didn't feel like it. I kept her pinned hard against the floor while she kicked and twisted under me. She thought I was going to let her go, but I didn't. I laid across her and pressed myself up against her struggling body. The leather skirt made a squeaking sound as my hard-on pulsed and spasmed against it from inside my briefs. Afterward we were both really quiet for a while. Then I whispered, "Gotcha."

GRETEL:

It wasn't like we'd never kissed before. I mean, jeez, we grew up together, we took baths together, we "kissed and made up" when adults told us to. We even experimented touching tongues one day after we'd gone to a matinee of "Summer Love" where we saw actors French kiss for the first time. I mean, why not? Who else would we trust enough to try mixing saliva with? It seemed so disgusting!

But that was then and this is now. Hansel wasn't letting me win anymore. So I had to get him back, didn't I? And lying there on the floor there really wasn't much I could use against him except my head—the rest of me was pinned motionless under his weight. So after he sank between my legs and I felt him buck and explode like an untethered pony, after we laid there really still and quiet and he still wouldn't let me up and he was arrogant enough to say "Gotcha" to me, I really had to do something to get him back. I stuck my tongue deep into his mouth. I thought it would freak him out and he'd have to roll off me. It did sort of freak him out. But he didn't let me up. Not at all. In fact he began to run his tongue around mine, in and out of my mouth, across my outer lips and then back in again for another sweet dip. And it wasn't disgusting. It wasn't disgusting at all....

HANSEL:
It was only a kiss, right? I mean, is that enough to get you disowned, banished, thrown out on your ass? There's no way the witch could've seen what was going on down there inside my underwear—my back was to her, and Gretel and I were clearly wrestling like we always had when we were kids, so the only thing she might have seen was the kiss. Which was really Gretel's fault, not mine. She was the one who slipped her tongue, electric and sweet like sugared licorice, into my mouth. Wow. All I can say is that bozo—her date—was a bigger idiot than I thought because Gretel really knows how to kiss....

Anyway, what was I saying? Oh yeah. What the hell was my evil stepmother doing in my room? She has no right to barge in on my private room without knocking and draw conclusions just because she saw me straddling Gretel's long, long legs....

GRETEL:
A kiss, a beautiful kiss, at last. And I don't care what anyone says. I don't care if he is my brother. I needed to be kissed like that. Ooh, I can feel it now, like a hot squirt of honeyed lemon oozing down there between my thighs whenever I think of how we kissed....

HANSEL:
She called it perverted. She called it unnatural. She said we would burn in hell but not before she had banished us from her house, and then she ran off to our father to rat on us and badger him like she always does, crying about how the neighbors would find out and she'd be arrested for harboring such ungodly children under her roof. Like any of this had anything to do with her! What would that ice queen know about how Gretel and I feel about each other? She is incapable of understanding real love. And then to turn our dad against us like that, to make him throw us out with nothing but a few bread crumbs! I never thought he'd go that far, but then I realized that her nagging had actually made him jealous! Jealous that we'd grown up and were young and vital and hot, jealous that I could hold his little baby girl close to me the way he never could, jealous that I got to taste the warmth and generosity of a really beautiful person like my sister Gretel instead of having to sleep with the cold old goat he calls

his wife. You know, if it weren't for her he might have actually been happy that Gretel and I were together that way. He knew we both needed love, deserved a little love, but she made him feel ashamed and jealous. Oh, why did she have to stand there watching? I swear, if I could just get my hands on that voyeuristic bitch I would push her into an oven and burn her to a crisp!

GRETEL:

So now I guess we're just permanently lost in the forest—no father, no mother, no school or stupid so-called boyfriends who don't even want to kiss a girl—just me and my wonderful brother. And this cool little empty cottage we found right in the middle of a clearing in the woods. It's really cute, like one of those gingerbread houses you read about in storybooks when you were a kid, you know? It looks like it was made just for us, like it was waiting for us to arrive or something because there was a warm fire going in the fireplace and tons of snacks to eat and Hansel even found an excellent guitar and amp set up there! Plus, there's this big room in the back with mats on the floor where Hansel and I can practice wrestling to our hearts' content....

———

That's where the diaries end. But it's a pretty safe guess they lived happily ever after.

he End

The Empress's New Lingerie

...there lived a very beautiful but very austere young empress named Victoria who was highly moral and severely strict in all her affairs, whether they be of state or of the heart. In fact, when it came to the latter, her stance was especially rigid: She demanded all potential suitors woo her in the most traditional and outmoded ways such as writing formal letters, calling on her for brief bouts of polite conversation in the company of a chaperone, and imbibing nothing more stimulating than a cup of tea during their intercourse. She also required these gentlemen to employ the utmost in courtly restraint when it came to physical intimacy or expressions of affection; she wouldn't allow even the mildest of kisses on the cheek until she'd secured a suitable offer of marriage. For this reason, despite her beauty and lofty station, the lady remained single and in firm possession of her virginity for many years.

No one knew how Victoria got to be such an ascetic, for she had not been raised that way at all! She'd had very liberal parents who tried to support their daughter's ripening from the innocence of childhood into the sensually charged years of adolescence. They enforced no curfews, vetoed no boyfriends, limited no experimentation that the young Victoria might choose to undertake. And certainly the community did not demand this brand of priggishness, for the peasants who populated her domain were a randy bunch themselves who'd always shared a bit of a wink and a nod of bemused tolerance for the naughty exploits of their rulers. In fact, libidinous temperaments were the only thing serf and sovereign had in common, divided as they were in all other ways by the grave disparities in wealth and status that characterizes such societies. So when her father passed away and Victoria was crowned head of state, the fact that she was such a prude served only to further alienate the people. Of course, deep down in her soul, Victoria harbored a dirty little secret that was unknown even to herself: She hated being the way she was. She yearned to be able to enjoy the fruits of her youth and beauty before they withered on the vine. But it seemed it was simply not in her nature to indulge this part of herself in any conscious manner, and so in her daily life she never crossed the line of what she considered to be proper.

Nowhere was this more apparent than in the way she dressed. She clad herself in plain, broadcloth underwear, which entirely covered her arms, legs, and torso and fully obscured the fact that she had a quite voluptuous body. On top of these unfrivolous foundation garments she layered frumpy, shapeless suits designed with prim high necks, modest hemlines, long sleeves, and bulky waists; the effect was to make her seem chubby, thick-middled, and altogether dour. To cap off this pious and invulnerable look, she pulled her hair straight back in a grim bun, kept her face scrubbed and cosmetic-free, and always wore sensible shoes.

One day, however, two fast-talking strangers arrived in town who changed all that. They claimed to be able to weave a cloth so extraordinarily fine that only the chaste and pure of heart could see it; all who were vile, vulgar, or lustful would find it invisible. As Empress Victoria so valued chastity and purity, they were sure she would find it the ideal fabric from which to cut a wardrobe. After all, if she had a suit made of this stuff she could easily tell who among her courtiers and ministers and ladies-in-waiting were innocent and high-minded enough to serve such a revered empress, and who were not. Intrigued, Victoria agreed to finance the weavers to the tune of a king's ransom in silver and gold, and they quickly set up shop in a little room off the village square. There they could be found, day after day, busy at their loom weaving the shuttle back and forth, back and forth, as if creating a complex tapestry. But to the wondering eyes of the passersby there was nothing there! No threads stretched across the loom, no yardage resulting from their labors—just the empty air being sectioned and sliced by the movements of the incessant shuttle. Of course no one dared reveal that they could not see the magic cloth, for to admit it would be to admit lasciviousness and impropriety and to risk banishment by the puritanical empress.

"I wonder how the cloth is coming," the empress thought one day. Then she remembered that the cloth would be invisible to anyone who was less than pure-minded and suddenly this made her a tad uneasy. Of course, she was sure she was as pure as she could be, but even so, it might be wise to have someone else look at it first.

"I'll send my honest lady-in-waiting," the empress decided. "She is my closest confidante and my right hand, and as such, I know her to be a very chaste and goodly young woman of honor."

So the lady-in-waiting went to where the swindlers sat pretending to weave their wonderful cloth. "Good heavens," she thought when she saw the empty looms. She opened her eyes wider and wider but still she could see nothing. The weavers begged her to come closer. Pointing at their looms they asked her about the marvelous colors and the splendid pattern.

The lady did not know what to say. "Can it be that I am so low, hewn of such lewd and lecherous stuff, that I cannot see the cloth? I must not let the empress know this!"

"Have you nothing to say?" the swindlers asked her.

"Oh, yes," replied the lady. "I am just so overwhelmed, you see! This is the most wonderful cloth I have ever seen! What an exquisite pattern! What brilliant colors! I will tell the empress at once."

"We were sure you would like it," the swindlers replied. Then they described the colors and the pattern to her. The lady-in-waiting listened closely so she would be able to repeat everything to Empress Victoria.

The empress was pleased; the cloth was turning out to be a fine investment, as it was purportedly of a quality beyond compare. It would undoubtedly make her a most excellent suit while it would also serve to assure her purity and worthiness. She ordered the weavers to increase their production so the cloth could be finished sooner and she paid them more gold for their efforts.

After a while the empress decided to see again how the cloth was coming. "It must be nearly finished by now," she thought. This time she sent her most honest courtier to have a look at it—a gentleman she thought to be beyond reproach in both thought and deed.

Like the lady-in-waiting before him, the courtier opened his eyes wide and then wider. But he, too, could see nothing. "I cannot possibly let the empress know this!" he thought, for the idea that a man within her court might be less than pure was even more distasteful to the empress than if he'd been a fallen woman. She would be sure to banish him forever. So like the emissary before him, he praised the beautiful colors and intricate patterns of the cloth. "I have never seen anything to compare with it," he told the empress.

At last Empress Victoria decided she must see it for herself. Surrounded by her ministers, courtiers, and various ladies-in-waiting, she went to the room where the deceivers labored over their empty looms.

"Is it not exquisite?" asked the lady and gentleman who had reported on the cloth to their liege. They pointed at the empty looms, certain that all the others could see the wonderful fabric therein.

Victoria stared and stared. "How can this be?" she thought. "I can see nothing! Oh, this is the worst thing that has ever happened to me!" And for the first time in her life, the dark and secret desires that resided below her consciousness began to slowly reveal themselves to her, much to her intense consternation. Could it be that she was not truly as pure of heart as she thought herself to be? If she found the cloth to be invisible, then she must be no better than the lowliest trollop; the idea made her dizzy.

"I must never breathe a word of this," she thought, "for my life will be deemed a sham and I shall lose all respect from and authority over my people."

"I must thank you," she said out loud, turning to the so-called weavers with a gracious smile. "I have never seen such cloth in all my life!" The rest of the company, who like her could see nothing, agreed.

The strange weavers then offered to make her Highness a very special gown out of the fabric—something sober and prim, suitable to her unsullied personage and appropriate for a ceremonious public processional. "For you owe it to your people, madam!" they said. "You must parade through the town proudly! You must show off the new royal robes that bespeak of your untainted heart and mind, to uplift and edify the good among your throng!"

"Yes," agreed her lady-in-waiting. "For all who see and admire the garment will prove their solidarity with your unimpeachable worthiness."

"True," Victoria said. But what she thought to herself was, "What of those among the crowd who may not share my rectitude? Will they not find the garment transparent?" And the very thought made her blush. All those dirty, grubby, grasping little peasants ogling her elevated untouched nakedness, her ripe loins, her superior breasts, and—dare she think it?—her perfect royal ass.

"I will do it," announced the virginal empress, "but only if these talented gentlemen will also make me special foundation garments to accompany and complement their excellent gown—something fashioned from ordinary cloth, of course, since the wondrous stuff they have woven is certainly too dear to waste on mere underwear."

The empress had bolts of flannel and broadcloth sent to the weavers so they could build the conservative undergarments she requested to wear with her new gown. But unbeknownst to their benefactor, the two con men sold these goods on the open market and in their place purchased rolls of red satin, coils of black lace, packages of the finest bone stays, and all manner of frilly ribbons, laces, buttons, and bows.

The morning of the processional finally arrived, and Victoria showed up with her entourage to receive her new wardrobe. The craftsmen first made much of laying out the gown cut from the magical cloth. They carried out a wooden hanger as if there was great weight hanging from its frame; they smoothed the place where the skirt would be and puffed up the imaginary sleeves.

"Isn't it magnificent, Your Highness?"

"Why, yes! It's quite unlike any gown I've ever seen. But where, pray tell, are my foundation garments?"

"Ah, of course, madam." And with a swift flourish, the little men whipped out a collection of the most sensual, delicate, revealing lingerie imaginable. There was a snug-fitting, strapless, red satin bustier that cinched the waist and pushed the breasts up high like voluptuous, succulent fruits ripe for plucking. There was a leather thong that rode deep in the crevice between the ass cheeks and slipped up between the vaginal lips to spread into the tiniest, little, heart-shaped emblem that cupped the tangled bush of the pubic bone. There was a black lace garter belt designed to sit low across her curvy hips, and a pair of smoky, sheer stockings that would caress her legs like the gentlest of midnight mists. The empress gasped. She had never seen underclothes like these and she was stirred and agitated and confused all at once. The ministers and courtiers who accompanied her were likewise shocked and silenced by the suggestive garments on display, and the whole room was hushed until the weavers finally spoke.

"As you can see, Your Highness—as anyone who is chaste and pure of heart can see—we have made you the most modest set of long johns to wear under your new gown."

Then they held out a pair of high-heeled pumps made from the blackest of patent leather, with spiked stiletto heels that gleamed like swords in the sunlight.

"And we also took the liberty of having the cobbler fashion a new pair of comfortable, sensible shoes for your arduous procession. Now hurry and get dressed, for your people await you!"

As if in a trance, the empress slipped into the dressing room with her lady-in-waiting.

"These are the most proper and modest undergarments you've ever seen, are they not?" she asked her friend.

"Indeed, milady," the maid murmured as she laced the empress into the boned bustier. "This camisole hides your shoulders, back, and chest with excellent coverage," she lied, pushing the empress's firm, round breasts into place above the cruel bones of the bodice as she pulled the laces tight. Victoria had never needed assistance with her undergarments before, and the touch of her lady's tender hands was thrilling. When they were done, the provocative brassiere overflowed with her flesh and her long, pink nipples stood out, exposed, erect, and pulsating, just above the lace-trimmed edge of the half-moon cups. The empress regarded herself in the long mirror and thought she looked extremely modest and proper, except for one tiny adjustment that needed to be made.

"Tighter," she purred, sucking her belly inward so her waist could be cinched as small as a kitten's neck. "Tighter, please."

"Of course." The lady pulled hard on the satin strings of the bodice and transformed Victoria's already tiny waist into a bending, yielding reed of almost scandalous slenderness. This was a tiny bit painful, but also sort of delicious, as her ribs were lifted to a floating position and the diminished oxygen to her lungs caused an intoxicating light-headedness. The rigid, inward pull of the bustier's stays made a fascinating contrast between the enslaved, minimized waist and the lush, fulsome bosom and hips that blossomed on either end; the empress had achieved the perfect hour-glass figure in her new lingerie.

"And the bottoms? Are they not perfectly prim and modest, too?"

"Of course, Highness. These leggings are of the most decent sort, designed to protect the virtue of a virtuous lady." She was now kneeling before her queen, fixing the leather thong in its secret place, snapping the lace garter belt across the soft, velvet plane of her hips and belly, slipping the whispering stockings onto her never-ending legs. From her intimate spot pressed up against Victoria's twitching pelvis, the young lady-in-waiting could smell the fragrant, earthy bloom of her mistress's flower and she couldn't resist a tiny, impulsive kiss on those hidden lips. Victoria pretended this gesture was as invisible to her sense of touch as the phantom gown was to her vision. But there was no mistaking the lurching movement she felt within. Finally, the breathless lady-in-waiting slipped the high-heeled pumps onto her mistress's dainty feet, and stood up. She then made a move like she was pulling a gown over the empress's head, although there was, of course, no gown to be seen.

"There," the girl whispered in Victoria's ear, with a tiny nibble on the delicate lobe. "Are you ready to parade before the eyes of a thousand strangers?"

"Mmmm," cooed the empress, almost in a swoon. "I am ready."

———

Oh, how she swayed like the wind-blown palms, how she undulated her suddenly liberated hips that spread out like fertile hillocks below the cinched waist and overflowing bosom above. The proud empress paraded among the throng, eager to reveal herself in her fantastic new gown to an admiring crowd. But the reaction among the peasants far exceeded anything she had imagined. They not only admired their stunning empress, they were driven to mad ecstasies of adoration. Men and women alike wept with gratitude as she passed by, displaying her new finery. Every couple of streets she would stop to ask if anybody cared to feel the careful stitchery of the elegant bodice or the rich weave of the skirts.

"Oh, yes, Highness, yes," they blubbered, and dozens of grasping hands would reach out at once to fondle the bare arms and bosom, the radiant buttocks and leather-and-lace-clad belly of their untouchable sovereign.

"Is the color not exquisite? Is the texture not superb?" panted the empress as she ground against their untamed caresses.

But the men could not answer, for they were so overtaken by the empress's new apparel that they soiled their own well-worn clothing right then and there with an unholy explosion of lust. Then they would sink in a heap at her feet and their aroused but yet-to-be-satisfied wives would have to revive them to make room for the next wave of ardent admirers.

"Ah, I knew I ruled over goodly citizens," she thought. "For even these simple folk can all see and appreciate my fine new gown. This proves they are completely chaste in thought and deed, and I am blessed to be the recipient of their pure and platonic love."

But then she spied a particularly handsome young laborer standing slightly apart from the writhing, whimpering, grasping crowd. He peered at the cavorting empress with a bemused expression from under heavy-lidded eyes while absentmindedly chewing on a piece of straw. She feared that if he were so unmoved by this display, perhaps he could not see the gown in question and was therefore not worthy to call himself her loyal subject. Much as she would hate to banish such a strapping young fellow from the kingdom, it would, of course, be her duty to do so were the laborer found to be morally lacking.

"Here then—you!" she commanded the youth.

"Me, milady?"

"Yes, knave. You alone seem to be indifferent to my dress."

"Quite the contrary, Your Highness," replied the lad. "I find your getup most becoming."

"Do you?" asked Victoria. "Then why do you not join the others in fingering and stroking the wondrous cloth or placing an appreciative kiss upon the charming bodice and elegant peplum?"

"Well," answered the cheeky fellow, whose jaunty attitude and cool demeanor toward her further aroused the already inflamed empress,

"I would be delighted to admire a well-made bodice and elegant peplum if, indeed, there were any. But I'm afraid," he continued, "the empress isn't wearing any clothes!"

"What?!" cried Victoria.

"You heard me. I said the empress isn't wearing any clothes! Just obscene and indecent lingerie, which, as I said, is most becoming to Her Ladyship's figure."

A hushed murmur spread among the horde. "The empress has no clothes, the empress has no clothes!" And those few who had been able to restrain themselves now climaxed furiously with the sudden liberation of this admission.

"Blasphemy! Heresy!" bellowed the mortified empress. "You, young man, simply cannot see the pure and modest garments I am wearing, which proves that you are nothing but a low and vulgar blackguard with lechery in your heart. I hereby banish you from my sight!"

"No," drawled the young man, who by now had stripped himself of all clothes. "You do not banish me, Empress. You embrace me, with all your heart and soul." He encircled the tiny cinched waist of the exposed empress and drew her toward his outstretched erection. Then he bent her over, right in front of the devouring eyes of the people, and slipped inside her dripping, virgin cunt, fucking her hard and long on the public square for all the world to see.

he End

About the Author

HILLARY ROLLINS is a playwright, screenwriter, and essayist who has contributed to *Cosmopolitan* and several book anthologies.

Printed in the United States
by Baker & Taylor Publisher Services